Future Girls

Book One
The Future Girls
Series

By
Catharine
Bramkamp

Eternal Press
A division of Damnation Books, LLC.
P.O. Box 3931
Santa Rosa, CA 95402-9998
www.eternalpress.biz

Future Girls
Book 1 of The Future Girls Series
by Catharine Bramkamp

Digital ISBN: 978-1-62929-167-3
Print ISBN: 978-1-62929-168-0

Cover art by: Dawné Dominique
Edited by: Avril Dannenbaum

To Andrew Hutchins
That's all, you know who you are.

Thank you to Damien Boath, my Podcast partner, who not only served as a close Beta Reader but has championed the book from the first day I started to write it during NaNoWriMo.

Thank you to my Beta readers: Michael Hutchins, Carol Collier, Beth Barany, Maura Harrington and Milly (who wants to be anonymous, but I can't do that)—you all gave me the most instructive and helpful feedback I've ever received.

Dabney Eastham, thank you for all your work!

Thank you to Andrew Hutchins who is always there for me, and supports all my projects as along as he doesn't need to read them.

Chapter One

Girls grew up in a hurry in the new state of California. Charity Northquest shuddered just reading *the rules for wives* from the *One True Word*. Once she read the words, she would be transformed from girl to woman, ready for marriage—like magic (of course no one said magic). It didn't make sense that mere words could change a girl. But she learned long ago that women did many things which did not make sense.

She could feel the congregation waiting. All she could see were the men lining the front pews. The women were relegated to the far back of the Temple, their heads covered by enormous hats, faces protected by veils. They softly whispered, trading recipes or indulging in trivial feminine conversation.

The *New Bible* was heavy in her hands. She scanned the page, she knew full well what she should say, Faith had said the words just last week, her friend Mirabella claimed her womanhood two days ago. Charity swallowed, she didn't dare delay a minute longer. Preacher Steve loomed over her, willing her to get it over with and return to the back of the Temple where she belonged.

Charity opened her mouth, but a shattering sound interrupted her. A huge rock bounced across the front of the room, past the pulpit and landing almost at her feet.

Startled, Charity automatically looked up to the preacher for instructions, interpretation and solace.

The mothers stopped their soft chatter. The noise, only a small bubble of annoyance a minute ago, surged into the jagged opening and flooded the surprised congregation.

The villagers. Charity shuddered and automatically stepped away from the shards of glass as if to distance herself from the problem. On TV the villagers were violent and brutal. The contestants in TV shows like *Survive Today* and *What Will You Do Now?* always panicked and ran when they came across a villager or servant on the outside. Of course the people were foreign and odd, why else would they stay outside the comfort and safety of the city?

Preacher Steve was a large man in a society of very large people. Yet, even as he stopped Charity with an imposing stare, he looked to the men of the congregation for guidance.

She ducked her head and hid her expression under her own large hat brim. Saved by the village riots: that wasn't something she had expected at all.

"We will exit, this way." The Preacher for the One True God gestured and on cue, the men rose as a single body and looked behind them to the rows of women. The women slowly rose. An adult woman, the Mother, didn't move quickly for two reasons: dignity and she was usually too fat to move very fast. Despite the rising noise and shattering of other windows, the women unhurriedly followed their husbands from the Temple.

"Come on, come on." For the first time the husbands seemed in a hurry. They gestured wildly at their wives and in frustration grabbed children and pulled them through the narrow exit doors.

Dazed, Charity carefully set down the *One True Word* on the pulpit and tucked her own copy more securely under her arm. She tried to scan the crowd, searching for her best friend, but it was difficult to tell the women apart, especially in the rush. Where was Mirabella? Fear coursed down to her toes. This was it then, not a carnival, not a celebration, but a riot, another dangerous riot.

Not even the well-trained company guards were equal to the sheer mass of people who, for the last four days, breached the city walls and flooded into every town and city in California. It was a celebration. Villagers dressed in their best outfits sang and danced into the night. She heard there were parades and even in some cities, huge floats. Everyone was ready to dance and sing, all to mark the hundredth anniversary of the Great Convergence of 2045 when all the religions joined together so peace, organized through the Reality Cloud, could reign. She saw today that despite the peace, one man's parade was another man's unruly riot.

Her father caught up with her. With another futile glance for her friend, she obediently joined her family of five out through the first exit, through another door to finally emerge into the old abandoned parking structure.

Sounds of chanting rose and fell, punctuated by the shattering of another window, maybe the Temple, or maybe a near by house. She was not certain since the noise seemed to engulf them as they hurried through the low-beamed parking structure. She searched the otherwise empty space for their preacher, their leader, but he was nowhere to be found.

Did he escape and leave them to fend for themselves? You don't leave your flock—just like in the Reality Cloud, you never leave anyone's avatar on the battlefield. Even girls knew that.

"Heathens!" Preacher Steve's voice rose above the babble of the villagers. "This is no way to honor the One True God. The anniversary of the Convergence, the Unification of all we hold holy!" He must have stomped through the front doors even as the last of the congregation members slipped out the back. His words burst over the angry crowd. Charity felt, rather than heard, a lull in the chanting as the big metal doors of the Temple clanged open. There was a pause, but then the crowd roared again.

She didn't know enough villagers existed to make up such a crowd.

"That was the last of the colored windows," Charity's mother commented. Father, with one hand pulling Faith and the other gripping Hope, said nothing. He merely pulled them all along as fast as they could run.

Charity was unaccustomed to moving this fast and her breath caught as she struggled to keep pace. Young ladies strolled sedately, took their time, did not call attention to themselves, but now everyone was running, albeit slowly. Charity was surprised at how many she outpaced, but it was wrong to be proud or to stand out from the many. They were all equal under the One True God, at least the women were. She took advantage of the chaos to pull off her floppy hat and drag at her scarf. Father had not slowed his pace and Faith was struggling to keep up. Hope, heavier than Charity, as was the fashion, wheezed next to her mother. Charity raised her head and looked directly up into the sky. It loomed low and gray over the city. Familiar houses seemed to shimmer under the diffused daylight.

The homes in their neighborhood were a purposeful jumble of architectural styles, created to reflect the whim of the owners rather than display a uniform cohesion. Half-timbered Tudors butted up against Craftsman Modern, and Mid-Century Glory. All the homes in their neighborhood were of the Beautiful Mansions program, fronted by lush lawns and gardens. Charity glanced at them, familiar, solid. But as she ran, the facades seemed to shiver before her, as if they were merely painted transparencies.

They raced to their own home, an imposing Victorian Mansion. Her father did not loosen his grip on her younger sister, even after they arrived at their own front walk. There were no walls around their home so they were still vulnerable. Charity glanced around and watched her neighbors disappear into their pretty homes.

A stab of loneliness tore through her.

* * * *

Just yesterday, Mirabella had walked with Charity from their school to the Temple. They had discussed the villagers, the danger of the riots, the violence. But Mirabella had been confident that her intended, Ray, would manage the crowds.

"The guards know what to do."

"What if there are too many? What if it gets out of hand?"

Charity guiltily patted the book she had carried in a deep pocket in her baggy dress. She had resented the baggy clothes, required just when her body was finally growing into something recognizable as female, but she soon discovered the garment was very handy for concealing things like small books.

Mirabella was the lively one and never, in all the years Charity had known her, bothered to hide the fact. Charity took the opposite strategy and nurtured a reputation as the perfect, pious girl. During school, as well as, in Temple, Charity kept her head bent over the *New Bible, the One True Word*. Her parents had presented her with her own copy years ago and she treasured it, never allowing either sister to borrow it. If her mother or sisters ever noticed what Charity was really up to, they never said. Every afternoon they trained their eyes on Preacher John or Preacher Steve and entertained themselves with their own thoughts, or whispered with the women sitting in the pew with them. It was an effective disguise, except it had completely backfired last week.

The Great Convergence celebrations and riots had pressured every man in surveillance and control. "We have problems at work," was all Father would say. It was all he could say. But Charity and Mirabella saw how erratic the power sources were. They knew the replicators were down more often than working. They knew that the Reality Cloud took precedence, it had to—it was what had kept the peace for a hundred years. But even the Cloud was over taxed by the riots and the villagers, even women knew that.

* * * *

Many of the Reality Cloud executives lived in the center of the Capitol on the shores of the Great Inner Lake. Charity was sure they were all safely inside their own protected homes, weathering the riots better than those in the Greater Bay Area. Some executives were more equal than others. She replaced her hat, not wanting to anger her parents who were obviously agitated and stressed. She clutched her bible more closely to her chest and glanced down at the earth, since there was no where else to look but down. The ground wavered; it was lush green, then brown, then green. She blinked and followed her family into the safety of their home.

The sheets were not even dry. Charity paused and took a few deep breaths eyeing the monstrous kitchen stove. She heard her mother calm Hope and Faith, helping Hope with her labored breathing. Father disappeared into his home office to enter the Reality Cloud through the home version, coded for his use alone. The house lights flickered. It was cold inside, so the heating system must have been compromised. It wasn't the first time the coal burning stove that mother insisted on was an advantage.

The lights flickered again, but held.

Charity took the last two pieces of coal and fed them into the stove.

"Nancy reported the Fabers in the market were down." Mother tested the sheets and wiped her damp hands on her pale blue skirt.

They used to just toss the dirty sheets and Nancy, their head servant, would bring in new from the market replicators every week, the old sheets recycled for their essential material. The family was probably using the same sheets over and over, on a molecular level, but it was still nice to have new.

Not anymore.

Charity glanced at the hanging sheets, no longer the original white. Just this morning she had helped her mother wrestle those sheets out of the big tub with a hot fire burning underneath, using up the bulk of the coal. Not for the first time Charity wondered exactly why burning coal and using water was better than employing the same energy to make brand new sheets. Still she learned long ago not to question her mother's methods.

Mother continued to focus on the sheets, as if they held some kind of answer.

"Charity."

"Did you see Mirabella?" Charity interrupted. "I didn't see her with her family."

Her mother took a breath.

"She read in Temple last week," Charity reminded her mother, just in case Mother didn't know who Charity was talking about. Charity didn't elaborate on her close friendship, women were, by tradition, were not encouraged to make close friends. But Charity had, and until today, had not been sorry.

"I know she did. It was just agreed that she would marry Ray Lewis. A good match, he is a Guard."

Why would Mother be concerned that Mirabella made a good match?

Her mother held Charity's gaze for a second. "She is gone honey." Her mother's faded blue eyes watered. "Her family can't find her; they're afraid she was caught in the riot."

Charity's whole body turned cold. Her first friend in school? Her first pal, her only pal, gone? But they all escaped! How could Mirabella be gone?

"Ray will be devastated of course." Her mother concentrated on testing the laundry and did not meet her oldest daughter's eyes again. "Of course he'll find someone else. He needs a wife to go into the Guards. All Guards have wives." Charity knew that. Any man who wanted to excel needed a wife and family. Someone had to stay in the home, feed the family, keep the electronics repaired, remember the One True God and his teachings, and instruct the children. If a man wanted to work in any part of the Reality Cloud world, he needed to marry, put his wife into a nice house and make sure she was blessed with children.

Warm water dripped from the sheets on her bare feet. They never wore shoes in the house, an old tradition. There used to be so much toxic material outside that the women finally stopped everyone from tracking it into the house by creating the rule—no shoes inside. Now it was a law.

Before Charity could say anything, Nancy came in through the kitchen door carrying a small marketing basket. She pulled her kerchief more firmly to cover her head and bowed. "I'm so sorry Mother, the lines were long for the fuel today, and the village riots stopped us from leaving the market."

"Takes a lot of electricity to manufacture the coal." Mother never raised her voice at the servants, she insisted on treating them as people, even individuals. Charity kept that eccentricity to herself; her friends, like Mirabella, reported that Mothers were supposed to berate servants and keep them in line, something Charity's mother never did.

Mother simply took the offered basket filled with only two day's worth of coal. "If only we could harvest wood ourselves."

"There are no forests." Faith flounced into the kitchen. She was twenty-one, an almost bride, and Charity thought secretly, impossible. Like Charity, Faith was a golden blonde, and blessed with elegant features. Her frame carried the extra weight of city dwellers, it was considered attractive.

For the last two months, Faith had relished being the center of attention as they all readied for her marriage to Nicolas Vandermere. The Vandermeres were new to the town, from San Francisco, but already well respected in the Company bureaucracy. Mister Vandermere seemed to come from nowhere, but Father had to respect his authority. The wedding had been set for tomorrow, but the riots and brownouts had interrupted the plans. Faith was not happy. Charity did her best to avoid her. Mother sighed and considered the huge fuel-burning stove. The family owned a small Faber of course, but the food pods were becoming increasingly difficult to obtain, even for a well-placed family like themselves. The only reason they weren't hungry, the only reason Hope was even well, was due to the dirt food mother grew in the back of the house. Charity never told anyone, not even Mirabella about the garden. But she had to grudgingly admit that there were many nights when her mother's eccentric gardening had kept them from going hungry.

* * * *

Only two days ago, everything was as it should be. If she had known, she would have been kinder, not pinched so hard.

"The RC has been fluctuating," Mirabella had announced as the two friends slowly made their way back from Temple. "I can feel it. Most women our age can feel it. Sometimes I worry that we aren't even real." She held out her arm. "Pinch me," she commanded.

Charity reluctantly took a pinch of Mirabella's flesh and dug her nails into the skin.

"Yikes!" Mirabella glanced down. "That's going to bruise."

"Then you'll know you're real won't you?" Charity shot back. They didn't dare linger on the street. But now that Mirabella mentioned it, the houses really did shimmer as they walked: sometimes revealing a plain one story home and sometimes turning into the glass and wood castles Charity always envisioned, always remembered.

It wasn't all that bizarre. They heard early on in their education that reality was one of two things: a shared community effort or an individual vision. The shared world community, represented by the one hundred-year-old Reality Cloud, was preferable. Women were proud to support such an instrument of world peace.

Yet, increasingly, Charity experienced the individual version of reality instead of the collective vision. It was not comforting. Oh, she knew about the individual, the adventures she read about in her borrowed books were fantastic. The heroines in those books made differences, helped their friends, made change in their worlds. But those girls all lived in the past, and so did the authors. She hadn't read any book written after 2050, almost a hundred years ago. What books could be found, were precious, even priceless. And something that priceless, needed to be shared.

Charity couldn't even imagine what would happen if she were caught. There were no stories about that.

She and Mirabella stopped at the corner. The narrow sidewalk was flanked by long strips of emerald grass. Charity counted five steps from the exact corner and stood very still for about a second until Mirabella joined her. Quickly, in the shade of Mirabella's hat, Charity dropped to one knee and plunged her hand through the green grass image that dispersed with her touch. She dragged away a heavy cement lid, quickly pulled out a small book and dropped the copy of *1984* in its place. She rose and with a practiced move, Mirabella stepped away.

It probably took them five seconds and this drop off was one of the more difficult ones. The drop off in the women's rest room in school was easier—there was no surveillance in the toilet stalls.

"I don't see why you bother any more. We're about to marry, and that will be the end of that," Mirabella complained.

"It's like seeing your own reality," Charity mocked her friend lightly.

"Well, it's just fiction, they don't even talk about things that are real, not like the reality shows on TV."

They engaged in this debate so often Charity didn't bother to pursue her opinion. Mirabella was always right in the end, mostly because she was the louder and more aggressive of the two friends.

On this they both agreed: their reality was shifting.

"What do you think is going on?" Mirabella asked, how long ago? Maybe a month or two.

At the time, Charity had assured her friend that it was just the surges that made the walls of their homes fluctuate, made the grass move as if a breeze had ruffled the surface, made both their fathers nervous and cranky.

At the time, she did not think there was anything to worry about.

She was wrong.

Chapter Two

Without Mirabella's impish observations, the walk to school was even more dreary than usual.

In the distance Charity could hear the rioting, which hadn't slowed or calmed all night. She wondered about attending Temple, would Preacher Steve be there to harangue them about staying true to the shared vision?

Charity stood before the heavy doors of her school building and scrutinized the place. She had been attending school here since she was five. The school boasted excellent test scores, and Charity contributed regularly to those high numbers. She imagined her academic progress was probably charted on a graph somewhere and monitored by a man just like her father—trapped in huge building, staring at a back-lit screen nine hours a day.

The school building was brick with white trim and a peaked roof. Just like the class videos about school. She concentrated on the building until the doors began to shift: wood to plain metal, back to wood.

"What is real?" she whispered. Of course she was being silly. Buildings didn't need to be real as long as they appeared interesting. Art was not real, just projected, as were stories. It didn't matter; what was real was what you saw or what you read. She fingered her *Bible*.

* * * *

Mirabella and Charity had met at the Old Women's Home when they were just girls. Months could pass without a visit, then suddenly, with no explanation, their mothers dragged them to the bare old hospital three and four afternoons in a row. It was not pleasant. Charity hated the smell.

For years it was their main topic of conversation. Charity and her best friend discussed the why of it all the way to school, and then all the way home as they walked sedately from Temple. Apparently it was a privilege to visit the old women. They only saw the wives of high C-Suite executives, but the honor was completely lost on the girls.

Last week, both Mirabella's mother and Charity's mother, along with the mothers of three older girls, Hannah, Honesty and Mary, had visited the Old Women's Home every afternoon between Temple and dinner, a precious hour. Mother was so distracted by the visits that Nancy had created dinner on both Wednesday and Thursday. Fortunately Father was too distracted to notice, and Mother didn't point it out.

"Have you ever talked with them?" Mirabella had once asked. Charity could see Mirabella as clearly in her mind as if Mirabella was a full avatar. Mirabella was forever fiddling with her hat and scarf constantly adjusting to achieve the impossible symmetry of adequate coverage and coquettishness.

"No, they're old women. Not even Mothers." Charity had scowled at her friend. "Why should I talk with them?"

Mirabella pulled off her hat, shook it and replaced it. "To learn. Listen, I just read at Temple, and you are reading next Sunday. I'll be married in a week, and in light of that I'd like to take this moment to ask, is this it? Is this our glorious future?" She mocked the tones of Preacher Steve rather perfectly.

Charity giggled with horror. "You aren't supposed to mock!"

"Oh please, he's an idiot." Mirabella dropped her voice, as if what she just uttered wasn't inflammatory enough. "The old women will tell you stories." Her blue eyes widened. "Fantastic stories of the past. Better than your books. I don't know how they know, but one woman told me mothers and daughters used to ride horses and drive cars."

"There are no cars," Charity countered automatically.

"I know," Mirabella twisted her scarf and tossed the long tail over her shoulder. "But in the old-fashioned days, people, even women, drove cars everywhere."

Charity was skeptical. "There is nothing on TV about cars. Remember the test on transportation? Cars pollute, use precious resources and are unnecessary as we don't need individual mobility."

"No they don't."

"Sorry, I always remember all the possible answers, that last one was wrong. Anyway," Charity sighed. "It's the pollution. Mother told us the pollution is the reason we live in walled cities and why kids like Hope can't breathe."

Mirabella put her hand on Charity's arm. "How is she?"

Charity shrugged, "she takes the medicine mother makes, but it's not helping." A vision of her baby sister, the last live child their mother birthed, so pale and always coughing, upset her so much she stopped talking.

Mirabella understood. Her only baby brother hadn't even survived infancy. No one said being a mother was easy; just the best thing a girl could do.

"So then, how do the old women know?" Charity challenged, desperate to change the subject.

Mirabella shrugged. "I don't know how they know. Who cares? It's kind of fun. They are nice, you just have to get over how they look."

Charity shuddered. "They are all so damaged. Preacher John said it was because they never married and had no children." Although she had no evidence that a perpetually single state engendered a lonely misshapen death, she didn't know any other outcome.

Preacher John also called these poor, damaged women handmaids, as in handmaids to the devil or agents of Socialism. But how did he know? She never saw him visiting the old women. Only women visited women.

* * * *

Good students knew the stakes were always high. If you fell behind and didn't test well a few days in a row, you were demoted to a lower class level where the testing was easier and your scores increased. Charity fought and studied to keep her status, and was one of the few girls still in school. Most demoted girls just dropped out.

Charity glanced at the empty seat to her right and struggled to concentrate on her final test. The Reality Cloud was launched in: 1990, 2015, 2045, 2046

Charity rolled her eyes. Trick question, 2015, but it was finally up and running on a world stage in October of 2045, when all the leaders and all the politicians could meet and discuss their differences without traveling anywhere—they met in their virtual world of their choosing. Right after the Great Convergence and the earthquake.

Name three California major exports, coal, wheat, oil, strawberries, Faber replicators.

Really? Strawberries? Never heard of them. She checked off the first three and moved on.

But even with stellar scoring, eighteen-year-old girls automatically graduated and ended their education. Out of pride, Charity took this last test as seriously as her first. She wanted to go out with a perfect record. She wanted her father to be proud.

"Be thankful," Mister Smith, her teacher intoned. Charity suddenly wondered what he had done to get the lowly job of teaching girls. Had he walked away from his surveillance post and missed a critical surge in electricity? Not made his numbers in identified terrorists? Charity studied the rotund man who looked a bit like the old illustrations of Santa Claus in a book she read long ago and reluctantly traded.

"Be thankful," he repeated. "That we are clean, safe and fed. Not everyone is fed, not everyone is clean." He glanced at the narrow windows, then back to the class of young women.

"Walk home with a friend," he cautioned.

But that friend was gone.

* * * *

Charity dragged her feet to Temple. Well, it was better than listening to Faith whine about Nicolas. Faith wandered around the house and sighed about Nicolas this, and Nicolas that. Despite evidence to the contrary, Faith was convinced that her marriage would lead to a better life than what she already had. Hope just coughed.

A gang of little boys tore down the street on roller skates. They were under eight. Boys entered the Reality Cloud at age eight, and from that moment, their lives would be entwined virtually with all the men in the world, the best defense to war and the best chance to hold on to, and keep, world peace. The highest placed men in the company participated in the Reality Cloud. Those who, for some reason or another, were demoted or downsized ran the electricity, the surveillance, the guards—unenviable positions all. And as of last week, her father was now part of the middle management system. It was a blow. Thank the One True God the Vandermeres were still interested in Faith marrying their son.

A dirty boy paused in his hell bent skating. He stopped himself and teetered on the dirt road next to Charity.

"Did you hear?" His voice was still high and babyish. "Drones found more rebels and terrorists! The TV crew is right here! We saw them!"

"The TV or the bodies?" Charity retorted. "You're just a baby, how do you know?"

"Snuck out." The boy smirked and beat his chest in pride. "Snuck out of Temple today, saw it—five real bodies! Wow, better than virtual, like the best game ever!"

Charity's throat went dry. She had never seen a real dead body, how gruesome! But the boys seemed surprisingly unaffected.

"They must be purging. Someone's got to take the blame!" He whooped and pushed off the curb and skated to the middle of the road.

"I wonder," Charity mused, "how he managed to sneak out of Temple?"

* * * *

That night Father looked drained. Deep black circles underscored his red-rimmed eyes. Since his demotion, he only pushed his food around his plate, replicated or dirt food, it made no difference to him, he ate none of it. The flesh and skin of his arms and neck sagged as if illustrating the burdens in his heart.

Her mother was silent as well. "Maybe it will help," she said quietly.

He nodded.

Charity looked from one parent to the other. Had they been in love? Or was it just a good match at the time, like Faith's? Charity snuck a glance at Mother, but Mother's expression was smooth and incredibly neutral. She did not mention their repeated visits to the Old Women's Home, tonight she barely made it home before Father.

When Charity was younger, Father had brought her to *Take Your Daughter to Work* day. She remembered how dismissive Father had been about the scores of men they passed on the way to his private office. Charity remembered the pale men who sat motionless before their monitors, all trapped in identical cubicles. The monitors flashed shifting graphs or images of crowds of villagers streaming out of the city gates.

Her father showed her the security monitors and the

warehouse where the men participated in the Reality Cloud. Of course she didn't see it in action, couldn't try it for herself. Father had delivered, with grave assurances, the various diplomatic negotiations that took place in the Cloud. "We work out all the great problems of the world because we meet in the Cloud—it's more effective than face to face." He smiled. "Well, it is avatar to avatar—the very same thing."

Now Father was one of those in the middle—a precarious position. Middle management positions balanced precariously between villager and executive. Another mistake and Father would be let go, or demoted. Regardless of what it was called, the whole family would suffer with him. That was the way.

She looked at her exhausted father. For the hundredth time she wished there was something she could do.

"Charity is eighteen. Faith is marrying in a week. I'd like to take Charity with us to San Francisco," Mother suggested. Father looked at his wife and grimaced. "To get a better dress for the wedding," she amended.

Charity was surprised. Her bridesmaid dress was perfectly adequate—long, baggy, and accessorized of course, with a large hat. She hadn't really given it another thought.

"No," he smacked his hand on the table, startling his daughters. Faith's eyes filled with tears, Hope's face drained of color.

"No, I signed the contract: we do not go out of order, we do not disturb the plan. And we do not leave the city, what would I say? That you have no confidence in our ability to keep you safe from villagers and terrorists? That we can't keep the peace?"

Charity could have sworn Mother rolled her eyes, but that was impossible, Mother would never do that.

"It will get better," his voice softened. "We are negotiating with a few of the Villagers who understand the Cloud, they can even meet us there. So it will be fine, the replicators will be up again, it will be fine. We just need to get through the carnival. One more week. If my team can make it smooth and seamless, maybe," he trailed off, talking to reassure himself or whomever was watching the family huddle over their dinner. Charity glanced up at the corners of the room—you never knew when it was your turn to be watched. Her father was right to be cautious.

"Very well." Mother bowed her head in a gesture of compliance and the girls followed suit. The Father had spoken.

* * * *

"They scare me." Hope pouted and folded her arms across her chest. "Make the servants do it."

"When you're married you'll need the food. The replicators may break, the lines may be too long. You don't want to starve just because of a silly chicken," Mother chastised her.

"They have sharp beaks," she repeated.

"And bad attitudes," Charity broke in. "I'll get them."

"You are spoiling your sister," Mother protested. "Hope won't always have you around to gather the eggs."

Charity paused at that idea. But then recovered, she may as well gather up these eggs tonight, spare her sister: one egg at a time.

Charity strode out past the raised beds of vegetables, past the two fruit trees and to the dirty, smelly chicken coop.

The scene was oddly real. The blind eye of the cam/monitor glinted in the diffused light.

Charity clucked and coaxed the eggs out from under each hen. She gathered six, enough for each family member. She knew the eggs would taste good, she loathed to admit they were any better than the eggs replicated on the family's Faber.

She held up her skirt with one hand and balanced the eggs as she negotiated the packed dirt yard. Ugly. The real world was so ugly.

Chapter Three

Charity brought in the eggs just as the lights dimmed and the walls shifted from a floral print to beige, back to stripes; a program mother had abandoned years ago. No one commented.

Mother and Father stood in the kitchen. Mother shook her head. "No, it's important we visit. You know it's our way of giving back."

Father frowned. "There is so much unrest." He trailed off. Not surprising or even disturbing Father didn't share more details. Charity knew they were lucky, sometimes Father told them more than girls should know, maybe that was one of the reasons he was in this terrible position.

A scream interrupted them. Faith pounded down the stairs and burst into the kitchen.

"Hannah's dead!" Faith wailed. "She was a bridesmaid! What if they postpone the wedding again!"

Father stepped over to the wall and swiped his hand over it. The news feed opened up. He quickly scanned it and then nodded.

Faith slumped against Charity who reluctantly braced herself to keep her sister from dramatically slumping to the floor. Fortunately Mother strode over and pulled Faith back to her feet. "It will be all right. I'm sure the Vandermeres will keep their promise. The wedding will happen the day after the celebration."

Faith did not respond. Mother shook her and made Faith meet her eyes. "Do you hear? Hannah was killed in the riots, like Mirabella. You just have to stay safe and it will be all right."

"Traveling to San Francisco is out of the question." Father closed the news feed and faced Mother as if finishing a very long discussion—or argument.

Mother released Faith and gave Charity a look Charity couldn't decipher at all.

"I know."

* * * *

"But father forbade it," Hope tentatively suggested the next morning. She stifled a cough and Charity automatically patted her back.

"No, he *suggested* it wouldn't be a good idea," Mother corrected her middle child. She helped Hope dress. Charity didn't like the look of her sister, she looked more and more gray as the weeks crawled by but mother forbade bringing it up. Since her father's demotion, there were no more credits for medicine.

"Won't Hope get them sick?' Faith adjusted her long beige dress and wound a long gauze scarf around her bright hair and lower face, just her eyes, red from crying all night, showed over the scarf.

"Doesn't matter," Mother repeated grimly. "These ladies are dying. They don't have long at all, the least we can do is see them off."

"The riots and the villagers are dangerous!" Faith supported Hope in the protest, but the mutiny was squelched before it even got rolling.

"We'll be fine, we're out of range of the riots." Mother was unusually confident. "Nancy will produce dinner. You aren't expected at school until next week. Come."

The Old Women's Home stood against the eastern wall, blocks away from the executive homes. Mother and daughters walked past increasingly smaller homes. The homes sometimes appeared plainly decorated, with only a single tree in each separate yard, then with another surge in the Cloud, the homes appeared larger and prosperous sitting at the end of curving paths flanked by full green trees. Charity blinked, preferring the pretty homes, but fascinated by the plain houses, like she was looking into their souls.

All her life, Charity was cautioned to never venture past the Old Women's Home. The only thing on the other side of the huge building was the wall and the guard towers. Beyond that was wilderness, the kind she only saw on TV...and even further—the villages.

Mother insisted the Home was a lovely modern building with large windows that let in copious light and clean air, just perfect for the hospice care these women deserved. But all Charity saw was a cement and tile building that was probably hundreds of years old. Landscaping around the Old Women's Home was virtually lush and green featuring tall waving ferns and thick low palm trees.

Mother walked briskly through the main entrance, a towering three story arch with no name or address. Her daughters reluctantly followed in her wake. She nodded to the attendants who bowed to her but did not acknowledge Charity or her sisters. Charity doubted any servant here at the Old Women's Home would recognize the three of them on the street.

Mother smiled but did not answer back. Mothers did not talk to strangers. That was another rule. Mothers were above everyone else. Charity heard this every day at 2:00 during Temple, she heard this every Sunday during High Temple.

There was no attempt to replicate comfort or elegance at the Old Women's Home. The Realty Cloud couldn't reach past the heavy walls and roof. As a result there was no illusion of comfort or décor. Rooms were little more than beds with TV screens suspended from the ceiling.

The old ladies languished in their separate rooms, immobile, white haired and exhausted, their withered arms and legs dangled uselessly against their thin bodies. The sun melted through the windows laced with chicken wire. It was hideous.

Charity would dearly love to just dump the cookies she and her sisters made by hand and run away. She was even willing to hide in the chicken coop—vile but private.

The halls in the Old Women's Home seemed longer than usual that afternoon. Faith and Hope trailed behind Mother. Faith was strangely silent, not joining with Hope's soft complaints as they made their way from room to room. Charity still couldn't see the point of their visits. All they ever did was smile and hand around cookies they baked themselves. Some of the old women accepted the treats as their due, and some were truly grateful. Either way, Charity never lingered.

"Water," a woman croaked. Charity froze. She hated when they called out like that. A servant or even a nurse would need to come, especially for water. They all seemed to demand water, like it was free or something.

Charity hesitated. There were no servants on the floor,

none that she could see. The light was harsh and cold in the hall reflecting from the low ceiling and bouncing in and out of the heavy open doors. The air was chilly, unmoderated. She could call out herself, but Girls, Daughters, didn't call out or raise their voices. Even when they read in Temple, it was softly.

She was at a loss.

"You there; can you pour me some water?" the old woman demanded.

Charity looked up and down the hall once more, just to be sure. She could fetch her mother. Mother was in the next room talking softly to a woman. Charity could picture mother's mouth close to the woman's ear, whispering just under the noise of the TV perched on a rack, hovering over the bed like a sentinel. Faith and Hope would be standing at the end of the bed, "like angels" many women had said.

Charity did not want to disabuse the woman of her assessment of her siblings so she let the angel comment pass. But if she asked either sister for help, she would look like some 'fraidy cat, afraid of giving a harmless old woman some water.

Mirabella would have given the old woman water. Mirabella would have asked questions.

The woman cried out again and Charity, remembering her friend's words, stepped in.

"Thank you, my dear," the woman croaked. To her surprise, Charity did find a glass pitcher filled with clear water. She poured the almost invisible liquid into a glass and handed it to the woman.

The old woman struggled to raise herself on one arm. The other, like so many arms Charity had seen, was withered, as if all the muscles and bones had been crushed, and the only thing left was empty wrinkled skin.

The old woman finished wiggling up on the bed and took the glass with her good hand.

"Thank you. I forgot how precious water is."

"How did you get such good water?" Charity asked, despite herself. She had always remained silent, like her sisters. Mothers did the talking. Charity took it as a lesson, this is what happens if you don't marry, if you don't become a Mother. Your end was lonely and unjustified. Perhaps these poor women were not even called to sit at the foot of the One True God, honored for all eternity.

"Where is your husband?" Charity blurted out.

"Not here," the old woman handed the glass back to Charity who carefully took it and placed it on the table adjacent to the bed. A small vase of flowers bloomed bright purple and red in the bare room and made a shadow of color on the white table.

"Is he dead?"

The TV show switched to one of the survivor programs. Charity didn't even need to look up to know the premise: a bratty boy is dropped off outside of the Towers and tries to survive in the wild without the help of the Cloud. No boy ever lasted past the hour length of the program. If the Villagers didn't kill him, the bare wasteland of the Far Valley would. Charity ignored the show.

The woman leaned back in her bed and shut her eyes. "I imagine he is. I should have followed him. But..." She gestured to the flowers and the water. "I had to come back. Silly really." She paused and glanced at Charity who stood rigidly, her arms clamped to the side of her long dress.

"Nothing really changed did it?" The woman's eyes were bright with intelligence. What was her story? Charity opened her mouth to ask, but Mother bustled in, the younger girls trailing behind.

"There you are. Helping?" She moved efficiently to the woman.

"How are you doing, Grandmother?" she asked with more kindness than Charity had heard in her voice all week.

"You should send her," the old lady said cryptically.

Mother glanced at her middle child. "She will marry. We already announced it in Temple. She read, well, almost read. She will have children." Mother included Faith in her statement. "They both will have children. That, too, is a future."

"Yes, but that takes longer." Was that sarcasm in the old woman's voice? It was shocking coming from an old person. Grandmothers should be kind and quiet, grateful for all the love and attention their family or caring servants can give them.

"Don't worry yourself." Mother fluffed up the pillows with a hard jerk and quickly ushered the girls from the room. Charity snuck a glance back. The woman winked, then apparently exhausted, fell back on her pillows.

Chapter Four

The riots increased overnight, spilling dangerously close to their neighborhood. The next morning school and temple were cancelled again. Everyone was ordered to stay inside except for the Fathers. Even her own father needed to access the surveillance cameras at the buildings in the center of town. There was no staying home for the men.

"Stay," he commanded, as if they were unruly animals. Charity watched her mother's back straighten. She said nothing. She kissed his cheek and waved goodbye as he made his way down the sidewalk to the center of town.

Once he was out of sight, she turned to the girls. "Come."

They hurried to the Old Women's Home so quickly Hope was in danger of being left behind. She rallied because there was no choice. Hope struggled to keep up with her sisters. Charity took her little sister's hand fearing that at any moment the riots could surge into their neighborhood. Their mother did not relent. Whatever it was at the Old Women's Home, they needed to be there right now.

Servants (of course they were villagers as well) rushed past them, not even finding time to bob a curtsy or nod their heads.

Charity did not understand the urgency. The home looked the same as it always had: old women, bare walls. Charity pulled ahead of her sisters and mother who were systematically stepping into each room, saying hello and mechanically dropping exactly three cookies on the clean table next to a water pitcher.

Charity was a fast walker and liked to get unpleasant projects over and done with as quickly and efficiently as she could. "If she were a boy," her father often remarked, "we could have used her. She would be brilliant in the RC."

"Don't be ridiculous." Mother's tone was harsh, as if what her husband said mattered, or was possible.

Charity chose to take her father's rare connection with her

as a compliment. She wouldn't mind being a boy.

* * * *

As Charity exited the fifth room on her crowded visiting itinerary, she heard raised voices. The unspoken rules of the Home were no loud voices and certainly no big displays of emotion. Charity was shocked to see Mirabella's mother. Just the sight of her engulfed Charity in a wave of wrenching sorrow. Mirabella's mother must have felt the same pain, but to display it so loudly!

Mirabella's mother was crying, yelling and hiccupping creating a bigger scene than anything Charity had ever seen on TV.

"Nothing has changed!" Mrs. Singh wailed. "The sacrifice, the credits, my husband!" Her voice echoed up and around the bare ugly halls. The servants scurried away from the two women, and quickly closed room doors.

"You don't know that." Mother's voice surprised Charity. She never raised her voice. And did she even know the woman? Wives didn't talk to one another much, maybe a little whispering during Temple, but mothers kept to themselves, raised the children, cared for the house. It was an easy life and required little thought or philosophy. The most real person in your life was the husband.

"You are here, I am here!" Mirabella's mother gestured to the walls, their hats, their shapeless dresses. "Then nothing has changed. How can that be? She was a smart girl, she was curious, you know that! You know how she got in trouble. She was perfect."

"You don't know. She may have made a difference. Your family is well-off, your husband still holds a good position. Maybe that was the change, you can't know what transpired."

"Then it was not enough!" Mrs. Singh snapped. "Not fucking enough! And what about Knight Industries? The electricity surges? The RC? Just, he will be," She choked, her sobs ending her fragmented statements.

"Come, the servants will create some tea." Mother snapped her fingers and a servant instantly emerged from one of the rooms and bowed. "Tea," Mother commanded, "we'll take it in the lounge."

The small woman scurried away.

"You did the right thing. It's the only thing we can do, the only way. We never know. One of them will make the change."

Murmuring other platitudes, Mother led the grieving woman to the lobby. Charity squinted down the hall. Where had they come from? What room? All the elderly looked alike to her. All the rooms were the same. Charity waited for her mother to disappear, and with only a brief thought to her own sisters, she dashed down the hall and searched for the correct room. The only door ajar was marked 509. She pushed the door and entered.

"Ah, Charity." A little old lady, barely ninety pounds, lay in bed. One arm and one leg were clearly withered. Her face a mass of wrinkles so deep her eyes were barely discernible. But they twinkled in recognition.

"Charity, don't tell me you don't know your old friend. It hasn't been that long."

Chapter Five

Shocked, Charity hovered in the door, unable to move.

"How do you know me? Did I bring you cookies last week?"

The woman laughed, a throaty, gritty sound, then immediately started to cough. She gestured for the water, in a plain glass pitcher and Charity automatically poured a glass and handed it to her.

"Crappy, but it will do." She drank it then wiped her mouth with the back of her hand.

"Damn cigarettes. Don't take up smoking, no matter what they tell you. Will make your final weeks just hell."

Charity couldn't take her eyes off the woman's face.

"Who are you?"

"Mirabella. Don't you recognize your best friend?"

Charity almost crumpled to the floor. "You died! You died in the riots."

"That's what they say, huh? I guess that way even if I did return, they wouldn't need to acknowledge me. They visit. I do appreciate that." She tipped her head. "Your mother took my mother out?"

"They are having tea in the lobby."

The old woman nodded and smoothed the blanket over her emaciated form with her good hand. Silence fell between them. Charity heard the footsteps of the attendants, the voices of her own sisters, emerging from one of the rooms into the echoing hallway. They must have hid there during Mirabella's mother's tirade. It wasn't polite to watch someone break down; you left them to themselves. She was surprised that her mother even approached the bereaved woman, but this was not an ordinary day.

"I don't believe you." Charity dropped her voice as she heard Hope demand to be reunited with her mother. A servant responded in low tones.

"Of course you don't. No one would, that's the beauty of it."

Charity listened as both her sisters walked to the lobby. She fervently hoped her mother had calmed down Mirabella's mother. It would be damaging for her sisters to see such an emotional display.

"Remember when I said that these women had great stories? About cars and horses and blue skies?"

"Blue skies?" Charity repeated. She searched the woman's eyes. They were really the only part of her body that was recognizable at all.

"Yeah, that sky was irresistible. I didn't get very far after all. Just stayed around the desert. Married a miner. We dug for silver in Virginia City. Met a guy named Samuel. He kept selling his writing for bad mine shares. It was pretty hilarious."

The Grandmother frowned. "Can you give birth to your own grandparents?" She considered it for a moment. "Great-great-grandparents. I went too far back, couldn't do any real good. Did have some children though, that's always satisfactory. They say children are our future." She leaned back and closed her eyes, cutting off Charity from her tenuous link with what could or could not, be her best friend.

Charity finally blurted out, "What is my favorite color then?"

"Pink, but all the girls say that." The other woman who may or may not be Mirabella didn't even open her eyes.

Charity smiled. "Mirabella always said that." She glanced at the bare room, the worn flooring at her feet. They didn't even make this kind of floor anymore.

"Then why did you come back?"

The woman nodded. "I'm dying; that's why I came back. We sometimes come back to check."

"Check on what?"

"See if anything changed." She lifted her hand but let it drop as if it was too heavy. "I'm surprised I don't have the bruise from that pinch you gave me. You're pretty strong for a girl."

Charity's eyes widened. She extended her hand to touch the old lady's arm, then pulled back.

"Did it?" Curiosity got the better of Charity. Mirabella or not, this woman knew something. Information that Charity realized was more important than learning about cars and blue skies.

Her eyes fluttered open and she looked directly at Charity. "No."

* * * *

Charity perched between Hope and Faith on the straight back pew and listened to Preacher Steve. He had replaced Preacher John, who was considered a hero for confronting the villagers in real time. She hadn't seen Preacher John since the riots. He had probably been promoted for his display of bravery.

Mirabella told Charity that she once saw something scrawled on a tower wall: "Some of the One True God's children are more equal than others."

She had read Orwell, she knew what more equal meant. She just didn't think it was possible in their world. What else was possible? She ducked her head and studied the book cradled in the cutout pages of her *New Bible*, but not even a mystery novel could hold her attention.

It dawned on her with a jolt that Mirabella had gone somewhere. Somewhere out, somewhere obviously interesting. And returned far worse for the wear. But Charity had a distinct impression that Mirabella was not sorry. Mrs. Singh cared, but not Mirabella herself. She was a wreck, she was old, and it was completely impossible. Yet.

"Let us pray," Preacher Steve intoned. "Thank you for blessing the pending marriage of Faith Northquest and Nicolas Vandermere and thank you for blessing the pending marriage of Charity Northquest and Ray Lewis. Not even riots and villagers can keep good daughters from fulfilling their highest calling."

Charity carefully shut her *New Bible*, her hands gripped the cover as if the book could actually save her. Marriage to Ray?

"Be obedient, be good, give back," the congregation responded automatically.

"There is only one True God. Bless the Great Unification. Bless the Great Convergence." Charity mouthed the words. She couldn't marry Mirabella's intended. Mirabella was still alive, at least that could be Mirabella. Charity needed to see her again but she didn't have much time. The riots surged and receded from the center of town to the outer homes. The noise lasted all day and all night. It could cover her own activities. How could she take advantage?

* * * *

Nancy silently served their dinner while Mother presided as if nothing had happened that afternoon.

"We will have you meet Ray next week. You can marry right after Faith." Father smiled with thin satisfaction, but his eyes remained troubled. "We are very lucky that the Lewis family will accept you."

"Yes," murmured Mother. "We are very lucky, this is a good life."

Charity looked down at her plate. The replicated meat was gray, as if the replicators had exhausted all the colors and now they were left with gray or brown. Still it was edible, they were one of the lucky families. Hope and Faith looked tense. For the first time Charity really looked at the family, sitting at their family table. Hope's blond hair seemed to be fading from bright yellow to a dull gray yellow. She was small, like Charity, unusual since most city dwellers were healthy and large with the look of the well fed. The bigger you were, the more replicated food you could afford.

Everyone was fair, even translucent white. Worse, both Faith and Hope had yellowing teeth, their hair and complexions were dull. When had they started to look so old? They were not even out of their teens.

Mother for her part seemed almost like the old women they visited. Father pushed around his food. He drank down the rest of his beer and pushed on the table to rise. "This will be good, your marriage. Mister Lewis is a C Suite, Ray will move up in rank in the guards, this will be good. Marrying you both to good families will make a difference."

"Of course it will help." Mother's tone was anxious and tense.

"Of course." He tried to smile at his wife, but didn't succeed.

* * * *

"We will bring you to Mister Lewis tonight," Father promised Charity on his way to the office the next morning. Then, as if he remembered something else, he quickly stepped to her and hugged her to him, hard.

That was all. He walked away into the soft gray morning light.

She would be married week after next. She stood at the door and watched her father, fear clutching her heart. She felt like he was walking into an abyss. She felt suddenly that she would never see him again. But that was ridiculous, she was as bad as Mirabella.

Charity turned back and regarded the kitchen. Her mother was rolling out dough, Hope and Faith helped. Nancy carefully fed coal into the stove. The lines for replicated fuel were longer and longer, even coal was in short supply.

The memory of the shimmering and Mirabella's insistence that it all wasn't as real as their senses told them, nagged at Charity. Not to mention the idea that she was marrying her best friend's fiancé. That was something for a TV show, not real life.

Charity staggered and gripped the door frame for balance. It was as her whole life flashed before her eyes

And it looked exactly like this scene in the kitchen.

Charity swallowed.

There had to be something else, something no one was talking about. Mirabella thought so.

"Charity, don't just stand there." Her mother finally noticed Charity in the door.

"What?"

"Come and help your sisters."

Charity obediently joined her sisters. They were trying to make pies for the wedding. But the apples were tiny and bitter, so Nancy was soaking them in liquid saccharine to get them soft and sweet enough to bake into a dessert worth the name. Hope was pretty handy with rolling pie dough, but Faith was clumsy with the dough and cried when her crust wouldn't work.

"Oh Faith, do have patience, this is important work to do, it shows that you know how to run a kitchen." Charity smoothed the crust and helped Faith start over.

Faith snuffled and wiped her nose on her long sleeve. "Why can't we just order the pies made? I bet if we ask the Vandermeres, they can just replicate what we need."

"Here," Charity leaned over her sister and helped her roll out each piece of dough so it was round like the moon. "See, like that."

"You do it well," Faith said.

"I've practiced," she assured Faith to avoid her ire.

"Ray's family lives around the corner," Mother started to say.

"I know, right next to..." Charity trailed off. Mirabella. Mother said nothing and neither did Charity, unwilling to bring up the scene yesterday at the old women's home.

What did Mirabella know? What could Charity learn?

She had until two o'clock.

Chapter Six

"Nancy," Charity hissed from the back yard.

When the family gazed out of the kitchen window, they saw a seasonal garden resplendent in perpetual color and foliage. Sometimes it was an English garden, chocked full with big cabbage roses and smooth gravel walkways. Other times the garden reflected the native Mediterranean landscape. Lately, when Charity remembered to look, the garden was decidedly tropical in appearance. But right now, the garden was nothing more than dirt with a tremulous garden scratched into the earth. Father never ventured outside, he was content with what he saw out the window.

"It's because he is so used to working in the Cloud," Mother had explained, a long time ago. "Most men just take what they see at face value, as the truth."

Charity glance up at the camera lodged in the corner of the house. It was disabled, destroyed during the worst sand storm in a decade. It had been a storm so severe it laid waste to the entire surrounding area. For miles the land was just bare dirt and sand, punctuated by rounded humps of cement that Father pointed out as old bunkers built during the Chaos of 2043 and now abandoned.

It was frightening, what a sand storm could do. But the land recovered, the green trees returned, the grass again looked lush.

Charity squinted at the camera. She had always accepted the story of sudden damage. Her mother had never been keen to fix it, or call in repairs. Charity wondered. But never mind, the black dead eye was another gift. No one would see her exchange with Nancy.

Charity rubbed her covered arms and thought for the millionth time that she'd love to feel the sun on her skin which of course, was impossible.

* * * *

‎‎ ‏

It wasn't as if the riots and celebration were a surprise. The Great Convergence had stopped, once and for all, corruption in the Government. It stopped inefficiencies and brought the free market to bear of every activity in the Reality Cloud. The One True God was pleased with commerce and betterment, of course he was. And since 2045—cooler heads prevailed.

Despite assurances to the contrary, even the C-suite officers of the Realty Cloud quietly predicted dire results from the anniversary celebrations. All the preachers, around the country warned of the impending chaos disguised as celebration.

Everyone knew it was their great misfortune to live in the time of the celebration.

"Madness." Father had lectured the girls, really, since Charity could remember. "It will all be madness. No one will be safe. People often become violent during these celebrations, these carnivals." His tone clearly said that his daughters were not those people. From the beginning Charity, Faith and Hope knew they would spend the week of carnival safely indoors, in their own house.

It seemed a shame really, parades, parties, people dancing in the street, that seemed like fun.

But there was a fine line between fun and chaos.

Tomorrow would be the peak of Carnival. The villages, just as the Preachers and Fathers predicted, had devolved into violence. The news was filled with all the terrible things happening in places like Brazil and New Orleans. But not here. They lived away from the center of the city, and even if it did not hold, Charity was sure she'd be fairly safe. Besides, all the dangerous villagers were busy.

At 1:45 p.m. the bells in the Temple rang to call the Girls and the Mothers to service. They would stay there until the Fathers came home at six o'clock.

Charity was early; the bells were just fading away. The afternoon was silent around her, even the chickens were quiet in the mid-afternoon lull. After another minute, she was hopping from one foot to the next. Where was that girl?

Charity poked her finger through the chicken wire at the big fat hen. The bird stirred but didn't get ruffled.

"I'm sorry. I am here." Nancy was breathless. She barely paused before pulling off her faded kerchief and handing it to Charity. Nancy's own blond hair tumbled down her back.

"Pretty hair," Charity blurted out.

"Thank you." The girl curtsied again.

Charity handed the girl her big temple hat, the one with a black veil hanging around the brim. Eagerly Charity pulled her long baggy dress over her head. Under it she wore another full layer: a long cotton slip and a full camisole with a bra under that.

Most servants just wore the camisole as is, with a sweeping patchwork skirt. Nancy stepped out of her patchwork skirt and handed it to Charity who slipped it on. She donned the kerchief, tying it behind her head. The bells chimed, five minute to go.

"Charity! Come on we don't want to be late," Faith called from the front of the house—she was too dignified to actually come back and fetch Charity, a distaste Charity was counting on.

"And miss the same lecture," Charity mumbled.

Nancy smirked and nodded. Charity twirled to test the skirt, it billowed around her like a bell. Nancy frowned and lifted the skirt. She tugged at the cotton slip.

"Yes, you are probably right." Charity pulled off the slip, so she was down to her long leggings and socks. The faded skirt fell better, sweeping the ground with its frayed hem and hiding her shoes.

Nancy slipped the petticoat under the dress, it filled out much better.

"Coming!" Charity pushed Nancy into the front yard.

"There you are. I hope you get it," Hope said with satisfaction. "I'm telling that you made us late."

Nancy, as Charity, just nodded her head, making the veil flap. Hope and Faith paid no attention. Charity waited until the girls circled the house and set off to the Temple. She hoped her bible was safe under her mattress, but there was no helping that, and no one ever entered Charity and Hope's room. She squared her shoulders and quickly headed in the opposite direction.

The streets were empty. The riot, or party was only background noise. Maybe the villagers were not as violent as everyone said? No.

No movement disturbed the dust that covered the sidewalk. The sky seemed angry with her for not being where she was supposed to be, and pressed down on her as if to hold her where she stood. She had never, ever, been outside at 2:10

in the afternoon. She was always in the Temple learning new chants and songs about the great Knights and how they saved all the religions by their fast thinking during the earthquake. How they moved the Great Unification talks outside to Union Square and saved all the leaders from being crushed inside the old hotel. Hearing again how the grateful nation states declared unanimously that the Knight family would serve as governors of California in perpetuity. How the free market reigned for the good of all.

Charity had never seen the Knights. She watched them on TV of course. The Knight Mothers dressed for Temple in exquisite pale yellow dresses, lavender for weddings. Sometimes the Governor visited Los Angeles but mostly he kept his family in Sacramento on the shores of the Great Inland Lake. The family had three boys, all younger than Charity.

Charity pushed back the kerchief and looked up at the sky. Gray. It was always gray. The afternoon was illuminated with weak passive diffused light. But the sun would burn them if the sky wasn't always so overcast. Everyone knew that.

Without her sisters and mother, the former with their short legs, the latter with her need for absolute decorum and dignity, Charity arrived at the hospital in half the usual walking time.

But once she reached her destination, she faltered.

What would she say to get in? Did she look enough like a servant? She smiled at the thought, she had never imagined she would ever want to look like a villager. But this was an emergency. She drew back and watched a servant exit from a door in the back, the entrance no more than an unmarked door flush against the outer wall. Charity scrutinized the servant, she was dressed in a kerchief and skirt similar to what Charity wore.

Perfect.

She waited until the girl disappeared around to the front of the building and then slipped in through the same door.

A long empty hallway stretched before her. No one had bothered to set up illumination back here. However, the few ancient lamps wired into the walls gave off enough light to prevent Charity from tripping on the uneven floor. The building seemed to pre-date the great quake which made it unique. Few buildings had survived the quake according to Mother. Blank cement blocks lined the hall, the surface broken every few feet by a door cut into the stone.

Charity moved forward cautiously, her shoes making no sound. She heard the squeak of a servant's black-soled shoe on the cracked flooring and paused holding her breath. The squeaking moved down another hall.

Charity's foot hit smooth dirt where the floor covering as well as the cement, had worn away. As she moved forward, she concocted the excuse that she forgot something in one of the rooms. No one would believe her, but all they could do was fire her and send her back to the village, and she'd escape before that. She was confident it wouldn't take long; she just had to be sure. That odd old lady knew something about Mirabella and her fate, and Charity was determined to discover what it was.

Charity hunched over and shortened her steps to look more like a servant. She wasn't a natural actress, not like the ladies on TV, but she hoped her ruse would suffice. She kept to the edges of the hall. She knew that the attendants and nurses, if they had time, often sat in the servants' lounge and watched a Temple Service on TV. Charity knew the only program on TV at 2:00 p.m. was *Temple Services* on every channel because once she was too sick to attend and has to watch Temple from home. Attending Temple while you were lying on the couch was much easier to take. She had slept through most of the sermon.

Luck was with her. She cautiously made her way to the closed lobby door, then backtracked, counting seven doors on the right.

All the doors were closed, the TVs in the rooms blaring the droning voice of the preacher.

She slipped into room 509 and closed the door quietly behind her.

For a minute she thought the old woman was already dead. The TV was turned up, the preacher bellowing about the sanctity of marriage and the exalted position of Mothers in the Kingdom of the True God. After they were dead.

Charity held her breath; was she too late?

The woman snorted and her chest began to rise and fall again.

"I'm back," she whispered.

The woman turned to her and blinked. It took Charity a full second to realize the woman couldn't hear her over the TV.

She reached up and turned down the volume knob. It never occurred to her to turn it off. You didn't turn off the TV until 10:00.

"It's Charity," she kept her voice as low as she could. "Now tell me what you know about Mirabella."

The woman smiled. "You're getting feisty, that's good."

"Oh stop. Just tell me." Charity's urgency propelled her to the edge of the bed and she unconsciously picked up the woman's good hand. It was blue veined and thin. The skin felt like the soft paper of an old book.

"Okay, Go. The old university is the easiest place. Go change this." She rolled her eyes to indicate the whole the room, maybe the whole of the city. "We don't have to live like prisoners, we don't have to just be mothers."

"But we're protected, we're safe, we have peace," Charity automatically protested.

"Safe. Prisoners. Same." The woman dismissed Charity's reflexive response. "Just go. I know this is hard and you don't understand. We aren't told anything at all, never will, by the way, and there isn't much time. You remember Hannah Vandermere? She did okay. I haven't heard about Mary or Honesty. But you need to go back. You've read books. You'll be able to cope. Just try to get to the Twenty-First Century, not far. The Nineteenth isn't where the change is."

"What are you talking about?" Charity glanced back towards the hall, but it was still empty.

The woman closed her eyes. "Please, for me. For Mirabella, if you will. Go."

A door opened and closed. Charity glanced at the TV. Probably less than an hour had passed. She had another two hours before she was discovered and brought down unspeakable consequences on her already beleaguered father.

Charity considered the TV again. The cameras panned the congregation. In the East the women wore hats of all different colors but like here, the women had flocked and settled at the back of the Temple building. Compared to the bareheaded men, the women's section looked like a brightly colored quilt.

It wasn't until just now that Charity considered the advantage of isolation, of big hats that screened expressions, covered low conversations. If Nancy kept quiet, and her head down, Charity's absence would not be discovered until the walk home. She could just hide behind the chickens, next to the well and meet up with Nancy at five o'clock. Done, no one will know.

Her adventure would not be discovered. All because of a hat.

A tingling ran up and down her arms and spread over her whole body. Go where? What did the old woman mean? She glanced back at the sleeping woman and almost shook her awake. Yet in the space of a heartbeat, the old woman's breathing had stopped.

Chapter Seven

The East Coast Preacher droned on. "There is a better place for you all, up in heaven, a marvelous place! Mothers will sit at the foot of the One True God. You will be revered! You only need to be obedient here on earth. Be good mothers and fathers. Be good children. And you will be rewarded in the next life!"

"What about this life?" Charity asked out loud.

But the woman couldn't tell her. Charity took one last look at the old lady and slipped out of the room. She counted the doors back to the servant's entrance all the while feeling terribly exposed. Every door, every sneeze, made her jump. Don't get caught. The refrain superseded the even more disturbing imperative from Mirabella or Mirabella's ghost—Go, go quickly. First Charity would exit the building, and she'd figure out the next step. Then she'd figure out what "go" meant. Did Mother know?

Charity exhaled with relief when she finally reached the long hallway. In a matter of seconds she was back outside in the blinding light. It was hotter than she expected, the sun burned her and made her blink.

"Round up." A tall Company Guard startled her so badly she almost jumped, but calmed herself to act like she knew what he was saying.

"Round up. All villagers must leave the city." He towered over her and she quickly focused on his boots, they were steel toed and shiny black. The boots gave her a turn. How to explain?

"Come with me." Three other servant girls were cowering behind him. He grabbed Charity's arm, squeezing hard. "No one should be out in the afternoon. It's a good thing I saw you." His voice was hard and as shiny as his boots. He marched her to join the other young women, one was softly sobbing.

"You know it's not safe outside, not with the carnival almost here." He pushed them past the Old Women's Home façade, past the buildings of the downtown, a place Charity had never been. Even thought she was terrified, she still glanced up at the three story buildings that towered over head. But she couldn't make out if the chrome and glass surface was a projection or the real thing.

She couldn't pull away. The guard was larger, more frightening and carried an enormous gun. He marched the girls past the tall smoke-belching towers and to an imposing gate flanked by two more guards. The sight of their long black guns and indifferent gaze protected by mirrored sunglasses paralyzed her. The man abruptly released her and she stumbled, catching herself just in time. She felt it would not be good to look too vulnerable.

"Look what I found!" The officer waved to the other two.

"Stragglers." One leered. His companion set down his rifle and advanced towards the group. "You shouldn't be out in the afternoon, all good Daughters are in Temple," he said with a sneer. "With the riots, no one is really safe are they?"

The girl next to Charity started to cry. Charity stepped back automatically, not wanting to be too close to the poor girl's emotional break down. What was going on?

The men circled the four young women like panthers circled their prey. Charity remembered something like this on one of the nature shows. Compared to animals, this circling was far more menacing. She had identified with the hungry tiger in the show. Now, she suddenly identified with the prey.

"You know what happens to girls who are found without their family men?" one guard asked harshly. He reached out and plucked one of the girls from the group. He pulled her towards him and began nuzzling and biting her neck. Her kerchief slipped off revealing her thick black hair. Like being stripped naked in public. The girl twisted her head, crying like the other two. Charity stood completely still, as if rooted to the hard earth.

"You," the other guard dropped his gun and grabbed the second girl. She, too, was stripped of her kerchief. He pawed at her breasts, slipping a hand under her corset and chemise, ripping them in his haste.

"You must want it; that's the only reason to be out," snarled their leader. There were two of them left, Charity and the poor sobbing girl next to her.

"I'll give you something to cry about." The last guard grabbed the sobbing girl and flung her to the ground. Charity couldn't even fathom what they were doing, how they were touching the girls. That wasn't right, she had only read...but before she could do anything, or even move, all three men had flung themselves onto their victims, awkwardly, but quickly, unbuttoning their pants. Charity was momentarily forgotten.

But she knew not for long.

Something loosened inside her. She would not be the victim. This would not end here. She steeled her nerves and did the only sensible thing she could: she grabbed a rifle and sprinted to the gate. If she stayed inside the city walls, even if she ran as fast as she could, she would be quickly found. But the outside was vast and confusing. She could hide behind a tree or something. She wasn't clear about her options—she just instinctively knew that once she was past the entrance point, she had a chance. Even the stupidest reality show contestant could survive a few hours outside the city. And all she needed was a few hours.

The girls behind her began to scream, but Charity knew no one would hear all the way out here at the edge of the city. Everyone was inside the heavy protective walls of their Temple. The screaming could be blamed on the villagers and the riots. The guards knew that.

She clutched the long gun and ran past the double check point, past the open gates and out.

She heard a grunt and a "Hey!" But she didn't pause; she couldn't hesitate. She couldn't risk looking back. She dodged around to the right to avoid being in direct sight of the gate. She ran along the perimeter of a high wall. Of course there was a wall, but whenever she looked out of a window, she viewed rolling hills, grass and lovely trees. From this side, the wall was just dirty cement. Her feet sank into soft sand and dirt, not grass.

She glanced away from the wall and her breath caught.

It looked like the aftermath of a sand storm. She squinted against the sun and made her decision: she turned and rushed straight out into the vast desert that looked like nothing she had ever seen.

Her brain couldn't take in the landscape. Where were the trees? Where was a good hiding place? She glanced behind her, but saw nothing, just a huge wall. The tower hovering over the gate, now out of clear view. She didn't have many more minutes. The Guards would be done by now, and she was next. She was merely prey to be hunted, like in a game.

As she ran she passed a round cement mound. She glanced at it but continued running.

Her side felt a stitch; her breath became more and more labored with each step.

She passed five more of the mounds before she realized some sported openings. They must be those underground bunkers created during the Chaos. TV shows were always a little vague on the Chaos and its causes, the majority of those shows spent more time extolling the current peace.

She circled a bunker, her breath coming in gulps, tears streaming down her face both from the shock and from the harsher sunlight. A dark opening. She heard men shouting as they, too, circled the wall.

She looked behind her, praying to the One True God that her steps were not visible in the soft sand and dirt. Just in case, she shuffled her feet before the entrance of the bunker and quickly dove into the dark interior of the cement sanctuary.

Chapter Eight

She hit dirt sooner than she anticipated and the jolt knocked the breath from her and stopped her sobs. The bunker was surprisingly shallow. The floor was only a few feet lower than the opening, but it was blessedly dark and cool. She gulped and steeled herself to think of the bunker as partially above ground. Underground was not good; it was death. People did not belong underground. Her stomach heaved, but she held on. She had to.

Charity crawled to the right of the entrance. She crouched in the darkest shadow and breathed softly in and out willing her heart to stop beating so loudly. She heard the men now. She gripped the long gun, not even sure which way to hold it, but it gave her some comfort. They must have finished with the girls and were ready for more, more of her.

She pulled off the kerchief and wiped her streaming eyes and sweaty face.

The voices were loud but did not seem to be any closer, thank the One True God.

"She couldn't have gone far."

"She took my gun!"

"Well, you can use it on her when we find her."

"She probably went to her village."

"Of course she did, you idiot. We'll go there."

"Any excuse right?" The guard laughed.

There was a pause, she thought she heard a sound, like scraping, like wind, but much louder.

"Shit, I'm out of here. You go hunt the lost virgin. I'm getting inside."

The two other men swore as well.

Their voices diminished as they retreated. Her relief was quickly replaced with a new fear. A sand storm. The guards were right, no one would look for her during such a storm and no one would expect her to survive one.

She glanced around in the dim light for something to block the entrance. She found some sticks and some rocks, but that wouldn't be enough. All she could hope for was the entrance was facing away from the direction of the storm.

She hunkered down, knowing instinctively not to emerge until the men were completely gone and knowing that she would be hopelessly lost in a dust storm anyway.

Ray would have lost two fiancées in one week. Possibly a record.

* * * *

It was difficult to discern between night and the dark of the storm. The wind howled and beat against the cement dome. Charity closed her eyes in the dark, but was sure she wasn't sleeping. She didn't know how long the storm lasted, but as soon as the wind died, she pushed away the sand and sticks and scrambled out.

From her vantage point, it looked like the city was covered with an enormous dome that glowed in the night. Charity regarded the attractive light, then turned and faced the opposite direction. Before her, the sky, the earth, and her path, was completely black. There were no sounds to beckon her and no light to guide her.

She fought the instinct to head back to the city and her family. The loser of those survival shows that Hope loved to watch always ran back to the city. He was always caught and killed just before he reached entrance gates. Because the guards were always waiting. And she understood better than before what it meant to get caught.

If she was caught, she'd sabotaged her marriage chances to Ray. The congregation would assume that what happened to those poor servant girls also happened to her. There was a marriage test that would prove her innocence, but it was done in only the direst of circumstances, like after a daughter and a son were discovered together and they were not married.

Even the taint of a test would ruin her. She would not marry and she could not stay at home. She would be downsized to servant: hauling water from the company replicators for some strange family or household...or she'd be banished to the villages, never to see her sisters again. Never to help Hope with the chickens, and every day, deal with the guards.

She had to find a way to reach her father directly. Could she find him through the Reality Cloud? If she could access the Reality Cloud, she could find him and explain. It was the only way to safely return. Even if he wasn't officially a member of the Reality Cloud now, someone would notify him—the men operated as teams did they not? That's what she learned in fourth grade.

But how to find an RC outlet?

Charity straightened her spine and turned her back on the city. Her eyes had adjusted to the darkness and she realized with a start that there was a light ahead, close enough, she judged, to reach on foot.

She headed to that smaller light, the brighter lights of her home receding with every step. The going was tough; the ground wasn't as bare as she first thought. Low bushes clung to the sandy earth and reached out to tangle in her skirt and rip at her thick cotton tights. She pulled the skirt as close as she could and hurried along, keeping watch on any movement that would reveal a guard, or worse, a villager on the hunt.

She finally came upon an old rusted water pipe, holed and crumbling, and she used it as a guide. It was a comforting but deteriorating companion. She hoped it would lead her straight to a village. It was an insane pursuit, but she didn't have many options. Even a village may have access to the Reality Cloud.

But the light did not draw her to safety. She stopped as soon as her eyes adjusted to the sight before her.

It was a village. But it was on fire.

She stumbled forward. The village huts were smoking. The roofs had already collapsed and the beams glowed like charcoal. She kicked something soft and looked down in growing horror. It was a body. She quickly backed away and ran back to the edge of the village only to trip over another body. By the light of the dying fire she realized it was one of the servant girls from the round up; waning light reflected off a patch of what was once beautiful hair. The body was covered with ash and dirt, most of the hair was matted and sticky.

"Oh no." Charity hunkered next to the girl and touched her cold face. "I'm so sorry."

Should she have stayed and defended the girls? What could she have done? The guards were big men, armed with intimidating guns, if she hadn't run...

Who would miss the servants? Who would read their names out during Temple? More important, who would read out the names of these guards?

No Preacher, probably not even the important Preachers who spoke in Sacramento, the heart of California, would. Mirabella's mother's voice came back to Charity. "Nothing had changed."

But change was bad. This was the best they could do. This was a life of peace. There was order to the days. Knight Industries ran everything smoothly and without stress. All the world's negotiations happened through the Reality Cloud. Women were protected and comfortable with the certitude of Temple worship the One True God for comfort and guidance.

Charity picked up a handful of dirt and gently sprinkled it over the dead girl. She muttered "Be obedient, be good, give back."

She rose and regarded the burned shell of the village. Villagers were dangerous. That's what she was told her whole life, that's what she saw on TV. She assumed it was true.

But she did not have much of a choice. If she wanted to get back into her own home, she had to find help in the village. They must have some connections or enough electricity to operate the basic program of the Reality Cloud.

Twenty-four hours ago she would have never dreamed of doing something like this. Still, twenty-four hours ago she thought the guards were there to protect citizens and servants alike. They were all equal under the One True God. She was beginning to realize that this may not be exactly right. Some of God's children were more equal than others.

She found another rotting pipe and followed it deeper into the countryside. Since she had no idea where she was heading, and no way of knowing if she was close or far, the walk was endless. It wasn't long before her feet hurt, her back ached and with every step the gun became heavier and heavier. After a few more hours, it became less a comfort and more a burden.

By the time she reached a smooth road, she had enough and ditched the gun. If she continued to carry it, she risked looking like one of the deranged village rebels, maybe just returning from wreaking havoc in the City. Without it, she was just a girl. She would have better luck approaching a village unarmed.

She dropped the gun into a rutted ditch parallel to the road. No, that was too close. She he picked up the gun and threw it as far as she could. Which, as she listened to it land with a thump, wasn't very far at all.

She rubbed her face with her kerchief and used it to tie back her long hair. For about an half hour, she relished swinging her arms as she strode along, but soon all the previous complaints returned two-fold and she felt even more exhausted.

Light began to crease the sky even before the sun appeared. She thought she saw signs of another village. Or maybe it was her imagination? Did it appear real simply because she wanted to see it so very badly?

The space around her opened up, the bushes had been cleared away and stunted trees pockmarked the hard ground. To her right were low buildings, much like the Reality Cloud buildings in her own city. The three story buildings clustered around what looked like a center square. Only in very dire circumstances should you approach a village. She straightened her aching back and stepped forward.

Chapter Nine

To her great relief, she did not meet with immediate disaster.

She was not accosted by the screams of women in pain, or the roars of angry men. The place lay quiet in the growing morning light.

More trees arched over a kind of central court. Green plants covered part of the ground around the houses. Charity squinted, but the green did not waver, in fact it became an even stronger color in the increasing light. Maybe there was strong Reality Cloud access here, but as soon as she thought that, she shook her head. Villagers did not depend on the Cloud. They were outside civilization.

Her spirits fell, but she talked herself into moving forward. She passed a tree, its broad leaves shaded the ground and the shadow was a cool contrast to the growing warmth of the morning. She wanted to pause in this weak diffused sunshine. When a Preacher talked about Heaven, Charity imagined it was covered with big shade trees like this one. It was the kind she saw in very old TV shows with plots that featured children who got in trouble because they climbed the tree in the front yard and couldn't get back down.

She hovered behind one of these trees and watched the tiny village—she counted about twenty little houses. There was a central well of course, this one covered with a roof, like a house, rather than surrounded by a locked cement gate. The small roof looked solid enough. She put her hand out and touched the surface, it felt like it appeared.

A girl Charity's age appeared at the door of one of the houses across the clearing. She glanced around, then approached the well. Charity considered that she didn't have much time before she would be discovered. So she took the initiative, just as Mirabella would, and approached the girl.

"Hello," Charity said, but then thought with horror, what if the girl didn't speak English? She hadn't considered that. She had walked for miles, and miles. Was there another language spoken in this part of the country?

"Good morning." The girl had a narrow face, darker than Charity's. She had brown eyes, a sign of a servant girl. All Charity's sisters and most of the daughters at Temple and school had blue eyes and all except Charity were much larger. Yet this girl was the same size as Charity. Maybe they had dirt food in common. You didn't get very big eating dirt food.

Charity stood awkwardly, not knowing what to say next. At least the girl didn't lash out at her or bare her teeth, or growl.

The girl set her bucket down and regarded the visitor.

"You aren't from the next village, are you?" she asked. "You're from the City. You're that girl they are looking for."

Charity was shocked. *How could she know? Way out here.*

The girl read Charity's expression and nodded. "Come inside, even here it's probably not very safe."

She quickly filled her bucket, hoisted it up with one hand and took Charity's arm with the other and escorted her toward one of the tiny houses.

The house was as small inside as it looked outside. All the furnishings seemed solid and real. The floor was just scarred wood with metal bunk beds pushed against the far wall. Brightly colored rugs padded the walls—the riot of purple, blue and red was shocking to Charity who was accustomed to soothing home programs. She averted her eyes from the confusion of color and focused on the family.

A mother and a father looked up as they entered. They were dark, like the girl. The mother held a small baby. The father was stirring something on a tiny stove that gave off no additional heat like the big coal burning stove at home. Charity didn't have time to consider this. She stood in the door suddenly overwhelmed, hungry and terrified. What would they do to her, these villagers?

"I think this is the girl." The villager carefully set down the water bucket and gently pulled Charity into the tiny room.

The father slowly nodded. "You're a long way from home." He poured the contents from the pot into blue, red and yellow bowls. Charity's mouth watered.

"I walked for miles," Charity blurted out. "Where is this place?"

"One of the State Villages." He nodded. "I'm John Nite.

This is my wife Martha, and the evil one there who brings in strangers as easily as water is Betsy."

Betsy curtsied like a good servant girl, but Charity sense the mockery in the gesture, as if the girl had talked with Mirabella and agreed with her. It was, surprisingly, somewhat of a comfort.

The father, John Nite, pulled out a bright green bowl and poured more of the thick stuff into it. "Here," he nodded to the table. He set down the bowls and gestured to the green bowl and the chair before it. "Sit, you must be hungry after..." He grinned; his teeth were white against his dark skin "...your long hike."

Charity didn't even care if he was mocking her, or if he would turn on her and kill her like all Villagers do should they find you inside their village. Villagers protected their turf, like a lion or a bear protected their lair. But if she was going to die, it may as well be on a full stomach. She didn't even ask what the stuff was. It was chunky and tasted mild without much flavor at all, but it would be filling.

"Oh here, Dad don't make her eat this plain." Betsy pushed a bowl of sugar towards Charity. Really? Just for the taking? Charity carefully spooned the sugar onto the pale cereal and took another bite.

"See? Oatmeal is terrible without sugar."

"You should be thankful," the mother, Martha, started to say. Charity grinned in spite of herself and Betsy grinned back.

"I guess mothers are all the same," Charity ventured.

"Yes we are, and your mother must be frantic with worry." Martha glared at her daughter, but managed a more comforting smile at Charity.

The full spoon hovered between the bowl and her mouth. "So, they know I'm gone?"

"A bulleting went out on the news this morning. Your father is, was, a very important man. The Lewis family is offering a reward for your discovery."

Charity grimaced. A few years ago her father would have been in a position to offer the reward, now it was her affianced family. Maybe Ray didn't want to lose two fiancées in a week after all. She didn't see her hosts exchange looks.

"She can't return, not now," the father said quietly.

The sugar didn't help the oatmeal anymore. Charity rested the spoon in the bowl and pushed back from the table.

She gazed at the little hut, cheerful and cozy, cozier than her fine house, more real at least.

"Thank you, your kindness was unexpected and generous. But I must be going."

"Where?" the father asked bluntly. "The guards will be searching for you."

"If they think I'm here, they'll burn your village." Tears filled her eyes. "Just like the Village next to the City, and they'll kill you." She gestured to Betsy. "I know, I saw."

"Oh dear." Martha handed the baby to John and knelt next to Charity. "Oh you poor girl. The guards." She couldn't finish, so she just hugged Charity who, for a moment, let herself be held and drew strength from a mother.

"Did they hurt you?" She glanced at her husband over Charity's head, but said nothing more.

"No, just the other servant girls. I ran away."

"That's impressive." John bent down and glanced out the window. Satisfied, he turned his attention back to Charity. "That you got away." He stroked his chin and considered the situation. "You can't sneak into the City, they have check points and we all need real time ID to get in and out. And your picture is now on TV. Congratulations, you're famous."

Charity didn't smile at that. She didn't want to be famous; she wanted to be safe.

"I thought I could contact my father through the RC, the Reality Cloud," she amended. "Do you have access here? Is there a place you can send me so I can get on?"

"If they think that the guards," the mother began, but her husband waved away her concern, as if he already made a decision.

"The RC, that's a good idea. Betsy. You can send her. It's probably the best outcome for her."

"Your village. The guards," Charity protested.

"They don't know you got this far. No one would imagine you walked ten miles overnight. And they're all pretty lazy. That village? The one they burned? It's not even ours, a TV crew built it about 80 years ago because they were too lazy to film anything further south and didn't have the fuel to get any further than a half mile from the walls of the City. That place gets burned, rebuilt, blown up, whatever is needed whenever a local show needs to depict Village life. Don't worry about it, but we do need to get you somewhere safe."

Martha issued one more hug and pushed Charity towards Betsy. "Take her, you know what to do."

Of course what Charity expected was to launch into another grueling hike. She glanced around at the tall cement buildings surrounded by snatches of grass and ground cover. What was out here that was so forbidden?

"It's dangerous outside." A fact, not a question.

"Yes it is, but not for the reason you think."

"What do I think?" Charity was curious. Betsy was dressed as a peasant, a servant, but she seemed far more mature and self-assured than Charity felt. Was she older?

"How old are you?"

Betsy led them across the open square, dotted with tall trees and two more wells. They must share the wells, instead of each family getting water from the Knight Industries replicators, or if you had keys and access, one of the few remaining ground wells.

"I'm twenty-one." She led Charity not to the outskirts of the village, but to one of the taller, more imposing buildings. It was ugly and grey like its neighbors. Charity tried to take in as much as she could while keeping up with her vigorous guide. The area seemed deserted.

"Where are the rest of the Villagers?"

"Busy," Betsy said shortly. She pushed hard against a huge door. It groaned, but gave way.

"Who is there?" A sharp voice rang through the hall. Charity thought the interior looked remarkably like the Old Women's Home. Was she back there? Was this just a dream and her stunted imagination couldn't come up with any virtual world that was even remotely better than what she had experienced in real life?

"Betsy, you idiot, who did you think it was?"

A door far down the hall clanged open and a shuffling figure emerged.

"Wake the dead then, will you?"

"In your case, yes." Betsy grabbed Charity's hand and pulled her along the hallway. The only sound was their echoing footsteps and the disgusted protests of the figure at the end of the hall.

"Everyone has already been deployed." The man rubbed one bare foot on his slacks leaving a dirt mark. He eyed Betsy. "Spoils already?"

"She escaped the guards at the City gates and made her way here." Betsy pulled Charity closer. "My brother, Jacob. Jacob, Charity."

Jacob was as tall as a Guard but not as well dressed. He loomed over the two women, but Charity did not immediately fear him. He had a kind face, almost as handsome as a TV star. He had hurriedly dressed and his shirt tails hung out of his faded worn slacks.

He whistled low and soft. "No kidding? You got away?"

Charity nodded and did not meet his eyes. She should not have been outside during Temple time. Served her right. Only very bad girls were outside during Temple. She couldn't even remember a time when girls did do anything but attend Temple with their families. She had read about it, of course, but all those adventures had happened well in the past.

"I couldn't save the others," she admitted in a low voice.

"Of course not! Those guys are brutes. Bullies. Bad to the bone."

He addressed his sister, "You don't have much time. The raid went well, they even got into the Knight compound, but they need to come back, and the grid is fluctuating like mad."

"Do we have enough power?" Betsy gestured to Charity with her head, keeping her eyes trained on her brother.

Charity lifted her head, the only light available came through another door at the end of the hall. She sensed the brother and sister looking at her, appraising the situation.

"Father said she needs to get out."

"Four in a row out and one back." Jacob glanced at the light now streaming through the far door. "Take a look, but I don't think we can help her here."

Chapter Ten

Charity swallowed. Bleakness fell over her. She had crossed something irrevocable. She had not saved the girls, her peers. All women were in this together, and she had run. She had failed the test of the One True God.

Jacob accurately read her expression. "The rapes are not your fault. The guards round up any girl they find and take advantage. They usually kill the girls afterward."

"That's terrible! They are here to protect us from," she faltered again.

"The bad villagers?" Jacob smiled again; Charity smiled in return. She couldn't help but respond to his friendly expression.

"Look, you'll have to trust us, bad press or not."

"There are no TV shows where the Villager saves the City dweller," Betsy pointed out.

"No," Jacob acknowledged. "There isn't a single show where the villagers win either."

He grinned at his sister and she grinned back. "None the less, I need to get her out, Dad said so. She can't stay here."

"No one can." He listened for something, but Charity heard nothing. "It won't be long."

"Yeah, that's what they said in 2045."

Charity had no way to judge the two before her. Were they sincere? She was here, not dead in the scrub bushes. Their Father hadn't harmed her, or driven her away. She knew she had little choice but to trust.

A gunshot fired off. Betsy and Jacob lifted their heads as if sniffing the air for information.

"Let's hope that's for you and not us."

What was going on? Charity was about to raise herself to her full five foot seven inches and demand answers when she was interrupted by an explosion.

"Shit. Come on." Betsy dashed for one of the interior doors and Jacob followed pushing Charity ahead. They ducked into a dim room. Jacob secured the door with a heavy metal bar. It looked like the classrooms on a history channel.

"Used to be the science building." He picked up a bag and shoes. A makeshift cot was shoved under a crumbling black board. A half a dozen chairs with narrow desks attached were piled in one corner.

"Do you trust us?" As Jacob hopped on one foot, pulling on socks and shoes, Betsy placed her hand on Charity's arm.

"Do I have a choice?" She had never been in a school like this—it was enormous.

"That's the spirit." Jacob grinned. He had a lovely smile. "Maybe you're the one to change things." He regarded her now he was fully shod. "Stranger things have happened."

He gestured to the tumble of furniture. The girls followed. He twisted the nearest table leg and with a groan the collection all moved together away from the floor to reveal a metal ladder.

Another explosion made Charity wince and reflexively duck her head.

"Down you go."

The stairs were hard and loud as she scrambled down as quickly as her shoes and long skirt would allow.

She landed into another classroom that felt to be the same dimension as the one above, but Charity couldn't see to confirm—it was pitch black.

"They kept all the computers down in the basement." Betsy left the stairs and walked confidently away to some far wall of the room. She flipped a switch. High noon light abruptly flooded the room making Charity blink, first because of the painful light, then in disbelief.

The room was packed with equipment the likes she had never seen before, not even on the news, not even on any history channel, not even in those cramped cubicles populated by middle managers like her father.

"My lab." Betsy opened her arms to both welcome her guest and encompass the whole of the equipment and the room.

"Your lab?"

Jacob flipped on a few more lights. To the right hung rigging. To the left, electrical panels flashed.

"You're a scientist?" Charity tried to get her head about the contrast. The girl dressed in a village skirt and kerchief was a scientist? "Do you work for the Reality Cloud?"

Betsy laughed. "Not really. I work for something much bigger."

"Then what do you do?" Charity turned to Jacob.

"I'm a coyote. I am the guy who gets you where you want to go. I do a little." He regarded the collection in the lab with some pride. "But Betsy is your girl."

Betsy studied the monitors, tweaking a knob here, swiping screens there.

"There isn't enough power. Damn."

"Enough power for what?" Charity finally asked.

Betsy ripped her fond gaze from the shiny, complicated equipment and regarded the city girl. "To go back in time."

Chapter Eleven

Charity's hand crept up to clutch at the solid metal ladder. She did not move. "You've lost your mind. You are going to kill me," she whispered.

"Maim you more likely. That seems to happen even with our best efforts." Betsy nodded. "You'll probably be okay from the Pub. That space is better. The energy is more consistent."

"You just said you didn't have enough..."

"Enough here, we have two portals, one here, not very glamorous but for an old university, somewhat appropriate."

An odd humming sound permeated the room and made her skin crawl. She shuddered and wrapped her arms around herself.

Neither Jacob nor Betsy noticed her discomfort. Jacob absently stroked his lower lip. "To be completely honest, it hasn't really turned out well at all. We thought that anything they did, any gesture, any word would change everything. You know, that whole butterfly effect. Turned out that's not the case. The future is more robust than we thought."

"You send women back in time." Charity tried to keep her voice steady, she did not want to sound like baby in front of them. "Why not men?"

He grinned. "Can't take it. Besides, why would they want to change anything? They have reality at their beck and call. No, no men. Besides after we discovered that appendages were prone to damage on the trip back, we didn't get a lot of volunteers."

"Appendages?"

"Sorry, you probably don't even know what a man looks like naked."

"Certainly not!" She forgot her discomfort, the odd crawling feeling all over her skin and raised herself up to her full height. "A good Daughter does not fraternize with any Sons until after marriage."

"That would include anatomy." Betsy didn't tease, she looked at Charity quite seriously as if she were important.

"You are more compact. All the really important parts are safely inside. Thus women. Not men. Not to mention the fact that you have far more to gain if you succeed and far more to lose if you don't."

Charity shook her head. "This is too much." She didn't add that she didn't even believe them. It was too fantastic, yet how fantastic was the new concept that Guards were dangerous and Villagers, helpful?

"Enough!" Betsy smacked a screen and turned to the two of them.

"Jacob, you need to take her to the Duck and Screw, it's one of the best places—and she'll get a head start over the others."

"The usual?" Jacob started to say, but was interrupted by an enormous explosion. The room rocked, but nothing fell, nothing seemed disturbed, except the siblings.

"That was too close." Jacob was suddenly sober.

"Just a precaution, they can't know," Betsy said reasonably. "Take her out of here. You can use the tunnels."

"Nope, the Economy Plus is down. We blew the last of our electricity getting everyone to Sacramento."

"The real train then. Just stop arguing and do it!"

Jacob turned to Charity and grinned. "She can be very bossy, see what you can do about that, okay?"

Betsy made a disgusted noise and rummaged through a far cupboard. "You have a hundred hours before it's permanent. Get back to the pub, before," she considered, "next Saturday. Here," she handed Charity a slender belt packed with both paper and coins. "This will help. Put it on under your dress, tie it as tightly as you can."

Jacob turned his back and Charity did as she was told.

"Okay then." Betsy gave her brother a fierce hug. "Be safe."

"Of course. Take care of Mom and Dad."

Betsy turned from the stairs and saluted her brother. "Of course. And you," she pointed to Charity, "change something."

Charity watched her go and felt gripped with the same panic she had felt just before she escaped the guards.

"We'll just need to do this the old-fashion way." Jacob quickly sorted through cards and folders on a steel table. He did not look at Charity but continued his work, muttering to himself.

"What are we going to do?" She rubbed her arms and watched the man warily.

He held up a blank pass card, "We are going to do all sorts of things. That's my job."

He winced every time a bomb hit, stirring but not shaking the lab too much.

* * * *

He worked as fast as he could. Both for her sake and for his. He didn't know when the rebels would return. He glanced at the computer monitor every few seconds looked for the signal, but no light appeared. Even though most of the village residents had retreated underground, he couldn't help cocking his head and listening for any sound the building had been breached. But he heard nothing.

Truth be told, the silence was even more troubling.

This was the first time he'd smuggled someone who had not volunteered, who was not at least partially vetted, at least partially in the know. An emergency. His father had warned him, trained him. There will be emergencies, and often, those hold the most promise. Damn, her timing couldn't be worse. He thought the four girls earlier would be enough, but maybe the city women wanted to maximize the opportunity: the power surges.

"Here," Jacob held up a bottle of dark foundation. "You may as well look the part."

Jacob smeared her face with the liquid until she was the color of sunbaked dirt.

"I know that feels odd, but try not to rub or touch your face. You'll need to blend in." Her nose immediately itched, but she resisted scratching.

He handed her a ratty scarf and she wrapped it around her head covering her blond hair with practiced assurance.

* * * *

Betsy wasn't the only smart one in the family. He had spent months creating an identification replicator, a laminating machine that would take the photo and the cards and glue them together with the press of a button. The IDs looked so authentic he was considering opening a business in multiple IDs, increasing the villagers' flexibility. Right now they could only enter the city once a week to sell their products, a slow, manageable trickle because they were the enemy, the unsafe. What if you could go in every day of the week? The coin would increase, they could barter for more building materials, create better tunnels and pull more water.

It would be better all around.

"No," Jacob's father cautioned. "The guards would recognize us after a time."

"Maybe we don't need to do it for very long?" Jacob hazarded.

"The officers and guards are smarter than that. They must know we're organizing. How could they not? There have been cautions about the celebration and carnival for years. They are ready."

Jacob was not so confident in the internal intelligence of the company. Sure, in the early years it had been as efficient as any new dictatorial government or new start up—all inventors and leaders. But as the years went by, middle management ballooned and inefficiencies were rampant—and easily exploited. But he kept his opinions to himself.

"Close your eyes." He snapped a photo of Charity with her head muffled in the scarf, make-up clogging her skin.

"Why close my eyes?"

"They are too blue against that dark skin, but so many people are startled by the bright flash—they close their eyes for the photo so it won't be that unusual."

The photo slowly emerged from an odd bulky camera. Charity watched in fascination. She had an ID, everyone did, updating it every two years as they grew until the women received one with her husband's name and photo attached—she could go no where without her husband.

"How did you get this?" She touched the camera tentatively.

"Stole it," he was matter-of-fact.

"Stealing is wrong."

"Yeah, there are a lot of things that are wrong." He glued the photo onto her card and pushed it to her to sign.

"Should I use my real name?"

"Sure, the conductors only glance to make sure we have IDs, plus you're traveling with me." He glued his own photo next to hers. "Now we are official, *mazel tov.*"

"Put these on." He handed her a pair of rubber soled shoes. "Your city shoes are a dead give away."

She did what she was told.

"Good. Now you're my wife. He made a gesture that looked like a cross in the air. "Let's go."

The sandals felt big, her foot moved easily in them, but they were comfortable. Not like her narrow, thin soled shoes which were pretty, but after trudging for miles in them she questioned their practicality. They were not made for walking. None of her shoes were made to hold up under any long distances.

"Just stay close to me," Jacob commanded.

A sudden explosion rocked the building. Things deep inside groaned. Something crashed to the floor.

"Okay, time to go." He glanced at the trap door in the ceiling, willing it to hold. He pushed away a heavy bank of old computers and replicators revealing another trap door.

"Another room?"

"Nope, it's all tunnels from here. Hope you don't mind close places."

* * * *

She minded very much, but Jacob pushed her ahead of him and forced her down an even narrow set of stairs. Before she could protest or scream, she was hurried below ground, like the dead.

He held her hand, squeezing assurances with every step. It helped to feel contact with another human under the dreaded earth. Thank the One True God there were lights. Charity brushed past low lights every few yards. The tunnel was narrow, barely the width of Jacob's shoulders. She stumbled over the packed earth, her scarf brushed the low ceiling, she had to hunch over and drop her head to make it through.

"What are these lights?"

"Electrical."

"Do you take electricity from your TV?"

He squeezed her hand but didn't slow his pace. "We use power from the plants, everything is electrical, stoves, lights, wells, all from those power plants."

She didn't understand.

He turned and smiled. "You can say that we steal the power too."

Her heart sank. "How?"

"We work at the plants, it's too dangerous for City dwellers, so we can just divert it from there."

Did her father know?

She tried not to breathe too deeply in the damp air, it smelled like dirt, but wet, not like the scratching that the chickens came up with, but rather something much stronger, more sinister. There was no avoiding it. She was now thoroughly underground. Like death, like everything she had ever heard in Temple. The living do not go underground.

Jacob drew up next to her and took her hand. "We won't be under here very long," he said in a normal tone.

"Won't they hear you?" her voice wobbled, she took another breath and blinked back sudden tears. The earth pressed down on her. She forgot to draw in air. Her skin crawled as if spiders had dropped all over her. But she followed. She had no choice.

* * * *

"Not this far under, no, and it's not like we're going to burst into song."

"What is this place?"

"Some of the tunnels are scavenged from old mines, gold, silver, coal, salt, you name it. They were abandoned years ago, so we use them. Others we dug ourselves, mostly to reach things like the electrical plants. Don't worry, no one in the city remembers these." He forestalled mentioning that there were tunnels directly under the city itself and a series of tunnels that linked them all the way to Sacramento. That was the problem, the High Speed train was down, their usual method of fast travel shut off because of the power. If anyone did survive the attack on the capital, they'd have to return on foot or by boat.

They passed another corridor snaking off to the right, a few lights illuminated the entrance, but it quickly disappeared into shadows. The ceiling dipped and Charity hit her head, a rain of dust settled on her shoulders. She tried to brush off the dirt, but she couldn't easily lift her arms. She shuddered and tried not to think of bugs.

"Death, death, death." The chant trailed behind her as she moved forward.

This Jacob could easily hurt her. There is no one here, no one to listen. Yet she followed, trusting him, sensing that he considered her part of a larger plan, and thus, would deliver her to her fate. And his.

They made a number of turns that Charity initially tried to count, but quickly lost track of. Finally Jacob slowed. The ground gradually rose and Jacob led her (thankfully) up circular stairs.

They emerged into another narrow tunnel, but this one had a higher ceiling and flaking paint decorated patches of packed dirt.

"Watch your eyes." He pushed open a door set in an alcove and they stepped from the dark into the late morning light that splashed across a wood platform.

Charity blinked and had to stand still to get her bearing, but Jacob pulled her restlessly along.

"Come on, look adoring or whatever the hell wives are supposed to do."

"Be obedient," she said.

"Yeah, that will be the day." He was suddenly in a rush. He yanked on her hand and she automatically followed. They were outside, on what had to be a train platform. Charity glanced around her as subtly as she could. The trains were packed, with both Villagers and men from the city. Some seemed happy, in a festive mood celebrating the Great Convergence. But others wore more grim expressions, intent on their business.

* * * *

Jacob recognized a couple men walking back from platform 4, they nodded and he nodded back, not enough to catch the attention of the conductors, but enough to acknowledge others. To not nod and engage was suspicious. Platforms One and Two were empty, they were just for City runs all the way from the coast, eighty-nine Clicks to San Francisco. But hardly any business people took the train anymore—the RC was too easy.

"No more real time," he grumbled softly. Jacob had always wondered about the trains above ground. The Very High Speed Transit worked pretty well, and very fast. Why had it been abandoned? His dad tried to explain that the tunnels were too difficult to maintain and surface travel was out of the question: too many tornadoes, floods, and sandstorms. "Of course, there wasn't much money in transporting anyone not directly employed by Knight Industries."

A shrill whistle made Charity jump. Men, mostly villagers,

leapt onto the train cars. A few City men pulled women behind them and clambered onto the train. It was not the smooth and orderly transition that was typical. Jacob glanced around for a conductor, but saw no one. All gone. Cowards.

He reflexively glanced at the platform for the train to Sacramento, 156 clicks away. The train was due here soon. He hoped there would be villagers on it, in case the tunnels had collapsed. He closed his eyes briefly, then returned to the matter at hand and pulled Charity to Platform Three and pushed her up into the second car. Ahead were five more cars all loaded with empty bins for food capsules. Inside the train car were rows of orange plastic seats, bolted to the floor. The floor in turn was sticky and black.

* * * *

Charity gingerly took a seat. Jacob moved her to the window and sat between her and the aisle.

"This is a faster train, about an hour."

"Where are we headed?" She peered out of the window at the platform and the station. Tired metal arches held up a short roof pierced with sunlight but she couldn't tell if the holes were decorative or the result of deterioration. Men shouted and ran to and fro, some glancing back at something Charity couldn't see. With another shout the train suddenly jerked out of the station, shuddered and clanged as it sped faster and faster.

The seats were crowded with Villagers, most were dressed like Charity and Jacob, and none paid the slightest bit of attention to the young couple. All whispered urgently, snatches of their conversation drifted to Charity, who kept her head turned to the grimy window.

"Three villages bombed."

"Just got out with my wife."

"The Capitol is in flames. They say the governor's family was killed."

"What a brutal response."

"Some were just there for the celebration."

Her seat rattled. She clutched the window sill to keep from sliding around.

"Suburbs are burning all over both Bay Areas."

Charity sucked in her breath. Jacob gripped her hand and squeezed so hard it hurt.

"What's happening?" She kept her eyes on the land racing past her as the train jerked and swayed. They shot past low cement buildings, big one-storied squares decorated with spikes and crumbling cement portions that in better times were second and even third stories. Smoke billowed out from the train engine and covered the cars like a fog. Green weeds shot up along the track, growing all by themselves.

"At this rate we'll be in San Francisco in less than half an hour," Jacob said.

"You didn't answer my question."

Long rows of green, punctuated by wells. Servants, and she supposed the Villagers, hunched over the rows picking something and dropping them into baskets. Dirt Food. Charity studied the people as they pulled and hunched and dropped. It didn't look like much fun.

Another crop flashed by, this one tall with heavy pods attached.

"Corn," Jacob pointed out.

At the head of one row stood a guard armed with a gun. His formal uniform was a grim contrast against the bucolic scenes they passed.

"Why a gun?" she asked out loud.

"We may have just started a war."

Chapter Twelve

Charity gingerly lifted one foot and then the other, the floor was so sticky it seemed to hold her in her place.

"What war?" she whispered.

"The one where we demand representation, just like in the olden days." He glanced around the anxious crowd. "And we may start fighting sooner than later."

"Why? Everything is fine."

The connecting door between the cars opened with a whoosh of air. Jacob squeezed her hand and she ducked her head to avoid eye contact. She tried her best to stay perfectly still, she didn't even dare look up. Fortunately the person shuffled by without comment.

"We'll talk later, there are too many people around here," Jacob whispered.

She nodded and turned back to the scenes flashing by the window. What she saw had to be real. It was difficult for her to get a fix on everything she saw because each time that door opened, she had to quickly adjust her scarf closely around her face and keep her eyes trained on the dirty floor. She breathed in the scent of fabric threads and dust, which, on three occasions, almost made her cough.

"Just keep looking down," Jacob whispered to her. She nodded and did what she was told. The green land faded into hills, they started to scale tall mountains.

"Okay, here we go." Jacob put a warning hand on her arm. "Close your eyes and fake sleep."

She nodded but she was suddenly so nervous she wasn't sure she could keep her body calm enough to fake slumber. She closed her eyes and strained to listen to the heavy footsteps pause, approach, pause.

"Papers?" A gruff voice demanded of the couple in front of them.

Jacob carefully arranged Charity's scarf over her lower face.

"Good job," he squeezed her hand just as the voice moved to directly over head. "Papers?"

She felt Jacob pulling out their passport and presenting it to the conductor.

"I need to see her face." The conductor's voice was hard and hovered yards above her. She tried her best not to cringe.

"She's my wife. She doesn't show her face in public." Jacob sounded just like a company executive or a preacher, she was impressed, but she held her expression still and kept her eyes closed.

"Her face!" the man bellowed.

Her eyes fluttered open, because really, no one could sleep through this exchange, even if she was innocent.

The conductor reached across Jacob and roughly pulled off Charity's veil. She gasped, then belatedly reached for the cloth, hoping the man towering over her wouldn't catch her hesitation.

Jacob was quicker. He grabbed the scarf, handed it to Charity who realized she also needed to keep her gaze averted, one look at her blue eyes and the game was up.

She turned her head as if mortally wounded and carefully replaced her scarf.

"I'll have your job," Jacob bellowed.

He really was good at playing an offended superior. Maybe he was as bossy as Betsy after all.

"Sorry sir." The man suddenly backed off. "Just doing my job you know? We are under orders to look for a girl, not your wife of course." He hesitated.

"My wife's family is from the East—all blonds." Jacob correctly read the guard's expression. "Of course," Jacob must have patted the man's arm. "We are all on edge now-a-days are we not? Hear any news from Sacramento?"

"The station is closed, good thing you're heading to San Francisco."

"Yes," Jacob paused. "Carry on."

"Yes sir; sorry sir."

The man shuffled past them, and didn't gain his previous officiousness until he reached the last seat of their car.

"That was amazing." Charity kept her head down, pulling the scarf over her hair and keeping her face covered.

Jacob patted her leg, "I learned it from my dad: the more officious and offended you act, the more quickly people back off. Remember that, you may need it later.

She nodded, her heart just starting to slow. Was there a later? If she did return to her family, her father's fate would be sealed. He would be banned from the RC and their family would fall destitute, forced to move out of the city to the village. And if that happened, what would he do? Executives don't work in the real world. Her father had no real life skills that she was aware of. The more she considered the situation, the more she realized that like Mirabella, they would say she died in the riots. She took a deep breath and almost choked on the dust in her protective veil.

The train plunged through a tunnel lined in white. Water dripped and dropped on the train, a counter point to the shaking and shuddering. They emerged into bare hills then plunged down onto a floating bridge that jostled the train. Water peeled away from the sides of the train, like that story of Moses. Fortunately it didn't last long and soon they moved around a corner, past twisted roads, collapsed buildings, big ones—ones that reached to the very sky.

"The City, old San Francisco. You've read about it right?"

Charity considered his comment, a daughter didn't just casually acknowledge she read, it was far more complicated than that. There were signs, rules, subterfuge. It was like a game she supposed, one the women played while the men worked in the Reality Cloud. "We saw a show about old cities, how they are dirty and bad. They are filled with crime and the homeless. People had to drive their dirty cars into the city every day—it was a huge waste of time."

"You didn't answer the question."

"There are many ways to answer questions."

He stifled a laugh. "Maybe you'll do all right after all."

She shifted again on the hard seat and felt the money belt tight around her waist. She knew about money, she just never used it...but Betsy was right, it was the only thing she really needed when she traveled.

Traveled, that was one way to look at it. The very thought made her throat seize up. What was she doing? She should return to her home and confess and do penance at the Temple and it really would all be okay.

The train jerked, shuddered and slowly pulled into a station twice the size of the one they left. This one was decorated with big windows filled with colored glass. The sky glowed through the glass. It was another color here, a blue that Charity had never seen, not even on TV.

She shivered as a stiff breeze caught her skirt as they disembarked.

As they exited the train, Charity kept her head down but no one really noticed her or bothered with her. Women with bare heads and long dresses rushed by her. Women in short dresses and huge hats brushed by her. Men dressed in dark jackets and matching suits that looked like what she saw on TV hurried past, as if no one wanted to linger very long in the chilly air or under such a bright sky. Five buildings towered over her, their tops almost six stories up, reaching up to the painful sky.

She didn't see it until Jacob abruptly turned a corner and drew her around one of the tall buildings.

Charity stopped, oblivious of anyone behind her and forgot to avert her eyes.

"What is that?"

"That?" Jacob glanced around. They were about to walk up the steepest hill Charity had ever seen. It looked like how she imagined mountains, but not even that tremendous slope held her attention for very long. To her right the mountain drifted down to a cluttered rim where, the sea, the real sea, churned and foamed.

She stepped to the edge of the rough sidewalk. Below her lay a kind of rolling hill, extending down in a vertiginous slope, directly to the waves.

"It's wild water, isn't it?" She gazed at the grey, sometimes green liquid that stretched out before her ending in yet another land mass that also consisted of rolling green hills. "Where did you get the green?"

"It's the bay, but the water is the same as the ocean; we can't drink it. And yes, the Water Department knows all about the sea. We've been working on desalination plants for centuries. Yet nothing has ever come of it. Too expensive."

She drew herself up. "You don't need to be huffy about it. I've never seen the ocean, what kind of reaction did you expect?"

"For you all to stop acting like five-year-olds," he muttered.

Emboldened by the new, Charity uncomplainingly toiled up behind Jacob as they made their way up the hill. Every other step her eyes drifted to the roaring waves, chewing at the bottom of the hill, hungrily eating away the hill bite by bite.

"Jacob," she said. "Your parents must have got your name from the *One True Word*. I remember the name from Preacher John's sermons."

He laughed, and turned to give her a hand over a pile of broken cement. Two men turned around the corner, staggering downhill as they pushed and controlled a cart filled with produce between them.

Jacob pushed Charity behind him and greeted the men.

They waved back, but didn't really focus on Jacob, or Charity. The unwieldy cart commanded all their attention and control.

"Not from the *Bible*." He waited until the men passed them, helped Charity over the last of the cement. "My mother found these old books that she thought were hilarious, a girl falls in love with a vampire and then a werewolf, and mom liked one of the characters so much she named me after him."

"From a book." Charity hadn't read that book, she was aware of course, that more books were written than anyone could read. She would dearly love to have that option, to access more books than she could ever read.

Jacob turned left, back towards the downtown area and they enjoyed three blocks of flat walking. "The big one left this area pretty unscathed. But you saw the buildings, it was,"

"Total chaos," she finished. "If it wasn't for the Knights moving the Great Convergence meeting outside to Union Square, all the delegates would have been killed when the Saint Francis collapsed."

"Exactly, their quick thinking and superior public relations made them the heroes. The government didn't even have the opportunity to defend their actions, or lack of action."

"It's been wonderful, we have peace, prosperity, everything we could want." She couldn't help repeating the words, she heard them often enough on TV and in Temple so they just appeared unbidden in her mind.

"If you believed that, you wouldn't be here," Jacob pointed out.

She scowled and followed him.

He turned the corner and headed for a half-timbered building wedged between a cement store with a bulls-eye painted on the side, and replicator station. A faded sign of a rounded duck with a screw superimposed over it swung in the cool breeze.

"Here we are," Jacob pushed open a scarred wood door with wavy purple glass inserted at eye level.

"A bar?"

"You don't know the joke? A girl walks into a bar." He led her through the door.

Inside it was cool and dark. She automatically rubbed her arms.

"The bartender says, '*what will you have?*'" Jacob nodded to, in fact, the bartender, who just glanced at Jacob but didn't hold eye contact. Jacob reached for Charity's hand and pulled her along the length of the long carved bar. "And the girl," he dropped his voice and glanced around the room. Charity stole a brief glance, but kept her scarf up around her face as if it offered some kind of protection.

Over the bar a huge TV screen played the latest Cloud Game—avatars competed on a long green field. They didn't get those channels on their TV at home. Charity was momentarily distracted by the running images. They looked marvelously real, she wondered what the game was.

Jacob casually glanced around, but again, didn't hold anyone's gaze for long. Charity saw there were a few people sitting at heavy wood tables, but couldn't really make out their expressions.

"Answers," Jacob pulled her around the end of the bar and towards the back of the pub. "'*Everything, because I'm not coming back.*'"

"That's a joke?" asked Charity. There was a rustling behind them, the bartender shouted something and Jacob lunged down the narrow hall pulling Charity behind him.

He raced to the back exit, pushed it open and then pulled her back into the building.

"Why you? Why any man, you have everything!"

He headed back to a door set between two toilet signs. His smile was cynical. "It's not just women. Villagers are repressed, fallen government members are locked out of every system connected to the Cloud, and they are all connected through the Cloud. Education is a joke, for you—testing, for the boys, video technique and battle skills. Frankly, if the world is not good for women, it isn't very good for any of us."

"So, it's for selfish reasons."

He nodded and pulled out a key and quickly unlocked the door and pushed her inside.

"Good," Charity said. "If you're doing this for yourself, it will be more successful."

"You really are just like my sister."

The utility closet was dark and more spacious than she expected, then again, what did she expect?

Jacob quickly closed and locked the door. Charity went still, her stupid heart was beating so loudly she worried that whoever was outside would find them by that sound alone. Like in one of the stories she read.

The sound of footsteps hustled by them. "They went out the back!"

A more enterprising person smacked open the toilet door on either side of them and then tried to utility closet knob.

Jacob shook his head.

"What am I looking for?" she whispered.

The running footsteps now left the hall. The shouting was more muffled now.

"I told you, we don't know. No one knows, but there are three girls ahead of you," he paused. "Two that we know of. You can team up with them, or just watch for them. You have about a hundred hours, then you stay."

"Stay where?" It sounded like a very bad fairy tale, and those were not real. Four days?

"In the past. Come back to this pub, we know that much. You must return to the same point where you started."

"Is there enough power?"

"You're quick, good. There should be, if someone doesn't use it before you. A hundred hours, no guarantees. Also keep your hands inside the ride at all times."

"What?" She wanted to ask why only one hundred hours. She suspected he really didn't know that either. He forestalled any more inquiry by pushing her into a space distinctly colder than the rest of the room. She felt the same buzzing she experienced in Betsy's lab. The sound made her dizzy. She focused on Jacob's shadowy figure, but he wavered like a spike in the Cloud, and before she could protest, she plunged into complete darkness and was abruptly sitting on her butt on a cold hard floor. All alone.

Chapter Thirteen

She rubbed her eyes. Loud noise filtered through a low beam of light roughly the width of a door. Charity scrambled to her feet and remembered Mirabella. She gingerly flexed her hands, both seemed to be working and whole. She pressed weight on one foot then the other, intact as well. She grabbed her breasts, which didn't extend that far, but a girl never knows. She patted down her hips, a growth? Ah, no the money belt, undetectable under her peasant skirt. She cautiously approached the door, even though her first instinct was to just sit this whole thing out in the dark room. She certainly could stay right here for a few days, couldn't she?

"Jacob?" she called out softly. But as she suspected, she was alone.

Did anyone write a story about a girl who stayed perfectly safe?

Gathering the frayed ends of any courage she had left, she slowly pushed the door open to reveal the hallway she just left. This hall was more lavishly lined in what looked like real wood paneling. To her left was the heavy barred exit door below a glowing red sign. She turned to her right and slowly made her way down the hall. She passed one door marked with an outline of a man and woman and a second door marked with an outline of a woman and man. The noise volume increased with each step. She rounded the corner and caught her breath.

Before her were as many people as attended Temple on a high Sunday. It seemed like there were hundreds of them: all talking, chattering, drinking and hailing one another. A man grabbed another man and kissed him on the lips, then ran away laughing. Another woman and man stood in the shadows pressed against each other. Charity reached up to rub her eyes, but realized quickly enough, that it would make her look conspicuous. She was supposed to stay low and not call attention to herself. As if that were possible.

She noticed immediately her outfit was completely wrong. The women here were dressed in tight dresses, shorts, and colorful tights. Three women sported fantastic hats that didn't cover much of their heads at all, but rose like birds to hover over their short cropped hair.

She may as well rub her eyes, her dress alone would give her away.

She was tired and starving. She hadn't really slept in that bunker, and now she was faced with an entirely new life, a new world, perhaps a dream?

Could she sleep in her own dream? Could she get a little food in her dream?

More than anything she wanted to wake up from this nightmare in her own bed with the TV on and her sisters softly bickering about the bridesmaid dresses. Even if she did find a place safe enough to sleep, she obviously would not wake up in her cozy bed. She would still be here. This wasn't a dream. It was a living nightmare, as if the whole Cloud had gone horribly wrong.

She caught the eye of a young man sitting alone at a far table. He quickly dropped his eyes and continued to fiddle with a half-filled glass. A man walked through the door and hailed the bartender as an old friend, but Charity didn't look that way. She wanted to appear cool, like she hung out in bars every day.

She felt, rather than saw another person approach from behind her.

"Say, did it hurt?" a low voice whispered. Her neck hair rose from the sound of the voice.

"What?" she barely whispered.

* * * *

"Let's hope she's the last of them," Dranit muttered under his breath. He glanced around to make sure the others had already left and his gaze caught on the man ordering at the bar. Dranit kept his eyes on the man even as he pulled out the phone to message Grandfather. He glanced at the girl, but noted with relief that she didn't make eye contact with the man at the bar—good. She looked around the room as if she had just come straight from Kansas or more likely the broom closet. Same thing.

He paused *The Princess Bride* and switched to the message application. He watched her take in the scene. Her eyes were startling blue and her hair was a magnificent golden blond. Natural, he could tell. She was much thinner than the others.

His finger hovered over the application, prepared to hit send. That was the deal. Over the last three years he had found five out of the seven. He should be congratulated, but all his grandfather wanted to know was why he had missed the other two. *My name is Inigo Montoya. You killed my father.*

A man, no one he recognized, suddenly popped up behind the girl.

She was dressed absurdly, but this was a city of the absurd during an absurd time, so she didn't look too out of place. Her blue eyes were the clearest, and most innocent he had ever seen. Why were the girls from the future so innocent? Ah well.

The man at the bar shifted, the man behind the girl whispered something that seemed to startle her.

Dranit abandoned the phone, slipping it into his jacket as he slid off his chair. He pushed up his sleeves in his best Don Johnson impersonation and quickly threaded his way around the tables to reach her before any one else could catch her eye.

"When you fell from heaven, did it hurt?" The man was loud enough for Dranit to hear.

The line made Dranit stop dead in his tracks. "That's it? That's your line?" He gingerly extracted the other man's hand from the girl's bare arm. "Seriously, you need to work on a better opening than that."

"I'm not as good as you." Under Dranit's cold gaze, the menace was quickly reduced to just a boy.

Charity was relieved and overly grateful to the tall man. She stepped away from her tormentor and towards the better dressed man with dark eyes.

"No one is as good as me." To Charity Dranit inclined his head. "May I buy you a drink?"

He positioned himself between the man at the bar and the girl, blocking his view of her and hers of him. "A beer?"

* * * *

This man was handsome, like the men on TV, dark hair, tall and slender, much thinner than most men from the city.

Her stomach growled and she blushed.

"Shouldn't we be introduced?" She was surprised by her own boldness, but it covered the sounds of her stomach. He unnerved her, but she realized that any man who spoke directly to her would unnerve her. After a generation of women marrying men they had never really spoke to, the direct approach was rather terrifying.

His hair was slicked back, long and she assumed styled, like the men of whatever century this was. Most men in her world wore their hair very short, because there is no real artistry in hair styles nor are their beauty salons. The women wore their hair very long and the men just shaved their heads. She supposed the male avatars in the Reality Cloud would look like anything the men wanted. Did that include the virtual women as well? She shook her head, not an appropriate thought.

To calm herself, she focused on the bar. The same riveted metal posts held up the same thick wood beams, able to survive a hundred years of neglect and indignity. *And earthquakes.*

She grew up wary of any stranger, but those days were over, she knew that now. "Impressive isn't it?" He had followed her gaze. She immediately grasped he was discussing the architecture—she hoped he was discussing the architecture.

"This used to be a printing press back in the early Twentieth Century, now it's a bar. Odd name, the Duck and Screw." He nodded to a loft that hovered over half the floor space. "That's the VIP floor. I can get you up there if you like."

She shook her head. "This is fine, thank you." She surreptitiously backed up a bit, just to feel the edge of the bar against her back. It felt solid. Was all this real? After the twentieth century, so at least she did not go back as far as her friend. What had Betsy and Jacob said? Go back to the twenty-first century, that's where the change was, that's where they had no information. As if she controlled where and when she traveled.

"I'm Dranit Knight." He offered his hand and she took it.

"Charity Northquest."

Knight—like the ruling governors, the company, the man, so to speak. She smiled as was polite, and he smiled back, his teeth even and very white. She felt like she had just met Big Brother. She should have never read *1984*. Was she even in

1984? She regarded his jacket and dark wash Levis. Maybe.

Dranit released her hand only to take her by the arm and propel her across the floor to his table. His hand felt warm on her skin. She knew she should not respond to him at all. It was inappropriate. But who was here to care?

He pulled out a chair and she sank into it. She felt like she had been running too far for too long; just as she felt after walking from the bunker to the village.

A servant delivered two tall beers and Dranit placed one before Charity. She took a sip and grimaced.

"I know," he sympathized. "All the pubs are running low. This isn't even fresh, just replicated."

"So, where are you from?" She couldn't gaze at her sudden partner for too long. She averted her eyes and focused at the activity outside the window. Pedestrians, bicycles, women carrying children or packages hurried past. Threading through the more determined pedestrians were revelers, easy to discern by their more impractical clothing and excess use of glitter and sequins.

"The City," he replied.

She didn't like the beer but it warmed her and put at least something in her growling stomach.

* * * *

"Where are you from?"

Her Renn Fair ensemble was different, he gave her that. She must be dressed prepared for the parades and parties. Something itched in his memory as he took in her dusty long skirt patched with bright fabric and soft cotton blouse. It wasn't a bad look, just a little out of place.

Dranit pushed his beer to the center of the table and leaned back in his chair, one arm carelessly flung over the back of the adjacent chair. This one was a little different, he couldn't put his finger on it, but there it was. She took in the surroundings, her fingers still on the glass and on the table.

"Oh, around here." Huge vehicles roared by making much more noise than the bicycles. Ah, cars. It looked like complete chaos to her, but no one else seemed very excited about the whole scene. She squinted at the sky, gray: that hadn't changed.

Patience and deliberation was not part of his family

heritage. Dranit was not supposed to dally, he was only supposed to pick up the girl, distract her with shiny things, shopping, alcohol, detain her just long enough for his grandfather to swing into action and Dranit's work was done. He was a key part of the family business.

Judging from her pallor and long unstructured hair, this one was from the same era as the three before her. How bad was the future for women? Dranit shook his head and adjusted the sleeves of his jacket. Northquest. He did not recognize the name. But that was no reason to be complacent.

He regarded the pretty girl. Tall for her era, and far more slender than the others. He still towered over her. Automatically intimidating. He had used that.

"So, you just..." He waved his slender hand. "...landed. Which makes me ask, 'are you a good witch or a bad witch?'"

She sucked in her breath and almost choked on her beer.

He quickly rose and slapped her on the back. "Sorry. It's a line from *The Wizard of Oz*."

"Thank you," she composed herself and took a deep breath. "I know. It's just where I come from witches are dangerous."

"I should hope so, otherwise they wouldn't mean much would they?"

"I'm a good witch."

"Good, then so am I."

She remembered the *Wizard of Oz*, it was one of the first books she found. There was a film, but for some reason it had been pulled off the air. TV didn't show everything, and the digital products of the Twenty-First Century were particularly problematic. It was called the dark century for a reason, it was difficult to boot up the old equipment and extract the information and history, in many cases, there were only ravaged books left to cover decades like the zeros and tens and those were in short supply. She knew more about the Twentieth Century. Nothing about the Twenty-First. Which was not helpful.

* * * *

Dranit returned to his seat and glanced at his phone.

A message from his grandfather asking where he was and what his plans were. He put it onto auto message and focused on his charge.

"I would think you'd have an implant so you wouldn't need to carry..." She gestured to his slender computer. "...that around."

"Like I need my grandfather in my head." He smiled. "The new, *new* thing is to disconnect, maybe I'll show you."

"Maybe." The beer warmed her, and the tension between her shoulders began to loosen.

The conversation lagged, long enough for Charity to feel sleepy. The bar was warm and the noise receded in the background, like a lullaby.

"How did you get here?" he asked oh-so-casually.

His question pulled her back to, if not to reality, at least to the here and now. She crossed her arms under her breasts and leaned protectively over her lap as if to cover her whole body. "Why do you ask?" She glanced up at him through her lowered lashes.

"Just curious." He didn't move or twitch. His arm remained draped over the back of the chair, his eyes were still friendly. "I mean if you came by taxi, I can give you a lift home."

She nodded and thought furiously. She turned her head to take in the scene and search for inspiration. She had no home, she had nowhere to go, and she was tired, bone-crushing, muscle-aching, tired.

Charity's mind raced, and the race track did not have much in the way of signposts. So, all those women, *all* those old women in the Old Women's Home had tried this. They weren't elderly at all, or at least they hadn't aged in her time zone. Either they didn't find the key or, as she was slowly realizing, they had. But how can you know? You don't, unless you return at the very last minute to see what happened.

They returned, it seemed, only to witness their ultimate failure.

Is that the whole of an existence? What if they hadn't failed?

Charity offered a weak smile. "I don't have a home here. I ran away." She could say it pretty calmly since it was the truth, and fortunately it seemed to satisfy him. She was glad she brought up the implant, not used much in her time—where would they go that anyone would need to track them? But if he assumed she had one; that was one less question.

"Sometimes a person needs to get away," he said seriously. "You look tired. I know a good place to stay. Do you have money?"

He gazed at her as if she was the only woman in the bar and she basked for a bit in the attention and focus then realized she needed to find a place safer than a bar filled with strangers. She fingered the bag of money, lumpy around her waist.

She couldn't just march around the street dangling a money belt clanking with coins.

"Before we go, I need to use the toilet."

He gestured to the same hallway from which she had initially emerged.

She nodded and chastised herself for her mistake, of course she should know where the toilet was, she had just come from there!

The bathroom was comfortingly clean, and every piece was real, not a projection. The toilet was already filled with water. She regarded the whole contraption and then used it, pushing the handle down and watching in wonder as the waste disappeared.

All that water just for her waste. What a great century!

She washed her hands under the automatic hot water, relishing the warmth and the feel of the odd foaming soap. Marvelous, just marvelous.

She glanced up and encountered her own reflection. The beer must be magical, her cheeks were pink, her eyes, usually flat, like her sister's, were sparkling somehow, the blue was a little brighter. She felt light-headed, but she guessed it was just from the drink.

Feeling as if she had over extended the typical toilet time, she unwound the money belt from her waist and extracted a handful of paper bills and coins. Silly really, but of course, much easier than RC credits, because she didn't need to register to use them.

Dranit said the bar was from the early twentieth century. And the building was old. She quickly sorted out the money. A few bills were dated 1890, that wouldn't do. She dropped them into the garbage. Then, on second thought, fished them out. Collectors. Maybe someone here collected old money. She slipped them into her pocket. Same with the money dated 1950. She left the two one-hundred-dollar bills dated 2090 in the belt and sifted through the remainder: a collection of bills dating in the low twenty-first century, and a couple shiny gold coins which could be very useful.

She silently thanked Betsy and smoothed her hair. It felt odd to be out without a hat, somewhat disrespectful, but she did not see any of the women wearing big all covering hats outside. She did not trust Dranit, as handsome as he was, but she needed his help.

Would it have killed Betsy to include an instruction sheet with the money? Maybe she could suggest that when she returned.

"I don't need everything, because I am going back," she said out loud, just to bolster her resolve. She didn't have much time, but she had to sleep!

The second she stepped from the toilet an explosion rocked the floor and shuddered through the old walls. She looked around as if the perpetrator or the cause of the sound was nearby, but all she heard was shrieking from both outside and inside. Patrons quickly emptied the bar, abandoning drinks and change.

"Come on." Dranit had quickly threaded through the crowd, pushing upstream. He grabbed her hand and tossed some green bills on the table.

She craned her neck, trying to read the numbers on the bills and calculate the date but he was too fast and too persistent.

Outside people pushed and raced past them. One man bumped Charity so hard she fell against Dranit. He immediately wrapped his arm around her shoulders to protect her and hustled her in the opposite direction of the crowd.

"Shouldn't we be heading the other way?"

"Need a car."

She twisted around mid-step to gaze back the way they came. A sign swayed gently in the cool air, a yellow duck with a heavy flat-topped screw superimposed over it.

* * * *

The man at the bar emerged just after they turned the corner.

"Damn," he muttered and headed in the direction they would most likely take.

* * * *

Dranit was right, within the next block an autocar barreled around the corner. Dranit raised his phone and the car rolled to a stop directly before them.

"It's probably one of the extremists. They are dead set against the Convergence. We've had bombings all week. Not the best way to gain sympathy." Dranit pushed Charity into the back seat of the tiny car and it launched away at a terrifying speed. She resisted the instinct to clutch the door handle with difficulty. Dranit was unaffected by the speed or the manner in which the car dodged around bicycles and running people and heavy pull carts. He tapped on this phone and the car took a right turn so quickly Charity was thrown against the door.

"Of course they set it off during rush hour." Dranit peered out the window. "It's a little hairy."

She looked at him in confusion.

"Sorry, I'm an aficionado of the 1980s; it's a hobby."

She nodded, but still didn't understand why traffic, or these vehicles, could suddenly sprout hair. She let it drop. It was slang, she remembered some of it from the old TV shows: jeepers, gosh. Again, a Slang to English dictionary, with a section for each era would have been enormously helpful. She made another mental note.

Charity gritted her teeth as the car climbed up the same hill she had just walked with Jacob. The thought of him gave her a pang. Had he been caught? What happened to the rebels and the villages? And Betsy, they seemed to think she was safe enough in the village, but what about the drones?

The car shot past huge beautiful homes, their RC projection intact and unwavering. The bomb obviously hadn't touched the RC. Although in Charity's world, nothing touched the Reality Cloud.

If the village had been raided, then it was up to her to change something, if only to protect her new friends. Not to mention her family.

The car finally stopped before an imposing gate. Dranit punched a few numbers on his phone and the doors opened. He helped Charity out.

All her life she heard that safety and peace were the best outcomes you could achieve. But what if that was wrong?

Chapter Fourteen

"Don't worry, no one is home." Dranit pressed his thumb on the edge of the gate and it gave way revealing a courtyard overrun with plants, fountains and miniature statues of animals all engaged in human activities. A beaver wore a hat, a squirrel sported odd wings.

"Grandma," he grimaced as she took in the menagerie.

Dranit placed his whole hand on the massive front door and it soundlessly swung in from his touch

"Place is empty, you don't need to worry about meeting anyone or making new friends."

Charity kept her mouth firmly closed, she did not want to gawk or have him think she was awkward or unsophisticated. Even though she was.

The entrance of the house led to a stairway that carried the eye upwards past a stained-glass window decorated with birds and flowers that reached all the way to the second floor far above. An enormous picture window just above the first flight framed a view of a magnificent orange bridge.

"The Golden Gate Bridge." He followed her gaze.

She stared at the graceful structure. Then turned to him. "You've been very kind. I really should go now."

He shook his head and ran his fingers through his dark hair. "It may not be safe yet. The bomb went off in the Financial District, close to the new Knight Cloud building. No telling if that's the last bomb." He paused, considering the bridge, "Or the first."

"Who?" Charity asked.

"What?"

"No, who is setting off the bombs?"

"Extremists, although one man's terrorist is another man's freedom fighter." He grinned. "Muslim, Jewish, even the fundamentalist Christians are taking a shot."

"Why?"

"They're protesting the Great Convergence of course. Some

are protesting the move to the Reality Cloud, but since their methods are surprisingly similar, it's difficult to tell what bomb is sending what message."

Charity shook her head—she was too tired, and not processing information quickly enough. The Great Convergence to the One True God was a historical landmark. It united the whole and created lasting peace, something that had never been accomplished. Had she landed in 2045? The year, maybe even the week, of the Great Convergence? Was this the history she was supposed to change?

"You can stay here for the night if you wish, you look pretty tired."

"Long trip," she admitted truthfully.

"Yeah, and there is a lot of pollen out in the fall, that makes people tired too."

"Pollen?"

"No bees. Nothing to pick up the stuff, so it coats everything and everyone twice a year."

October, she was days away from the Great Convergence and...

She met Dranit's eyes. She should warn him. He had been kind to her. Yet why would he believe her? Not even in her time could they predict earthquakes. He'd think she was a lunatic, she wasn't too sure about her own stability herself. Plus, she couldn't afford to be locked away, she needed to be free. Even if it meant being uncomfortable.

"I don't think I should stay here. Is there a hotel?" She would love to stay in this pretty house, relax into a real bed and see this man the next morning. But it did not feel right, and all she had to work with at this point was her gut.

Dranit pulled out his phone, frowned and slid it back into an inside pocket of his jacket.

"The crowds should be a bit thinner. Wait." He pulled out the phone again and grinned when he saw her expression. "I know, it should all be in my eyes, just ask and you have your information. But I didn't want to go through the procedure and my grandfather never insisted." He held up the slender devise. "I'm tethered to this, and it doesn't power off. That's just one down side."

She nodded, understanding just enough to not look like an idiot.

"The riots have moved, I can take you to Bob's place."

He led her back down the hill on foot. She was fascinated by the restaurants advertising both home grown and replicated meals, the cluttered store windows, filled with pre-created goods.

They marched past a number of buildings advertising rooms for the night. Dranit paused at one, glanced at her, then moved on.

"Bob's is the best choice. He isn't much for surveillance, so you should have some privacy." He squinted at her. "That's what you want, right?"

She nodded, what she wanted was one good rest and an idea of how the hell she was supposed to interfere with something as huge and enormous as the Great Convergence. No wonder the girls before her just called it quits and searched out for a life anywhere they could find one.

Dranit finally stopped at a cement block building that was almost as unattractive as the Old Women's Home. Once they stepped through the gate she saw that an enormous lawn and garden filled the center space open to the sky. Tall ferns and big tubs of leafy trees lined a narrow walkway leading doors on a first floor and a walkway and doors on the second floor.

"Why, this is lovely!"

Dranit pushed open glass door leading to a small office. "Bob created the garden when self-drive cars were banned from the City. May as well make it attractive."

The man, she assumed Bob, stood behind a tall counter. He was dressed in a white shirt that was grimy from either pollution or wear. He smoothed the thin strands on his head and greeted Dranit.

"A room for a week," Dranit ordered.

Charity opened her mouth to correct him, she only needed four days, then stopped.

The man pushed a paper-based log book across the desk. Dranit stepped back and indicated that Charity should sign the book. She wrote her first name but hesitated over the second. Should she leave a written record? Did this matter? Suddenly she was overwhelmed with the idea that every move she made, everything she did could matter. What was the one small thing that could change everything? Then again, didn't Betsy say that the future was more durable than anyone thought?

Oh, what the hell, she thought uncharacteristically, and

signed in. The man pulled the ledger away, firmly shut it, and slid the log book under the counter. He waited. Charity waited.

Then she realized what he needed.

She nodded and pulled out her bills. She handed a $500.00 note to him. His eyes grew large even as he pocketed it. "This way, Miss."

Dranit trailed behind as the man led Charity to room 5 on the second floor. Dranit hung back and allowed Charity to enter.

"I'll let you settle in," he said and withdrew.

Charity immediately pulled open the rough curtains and gazed down at the courtyard. Through the leaves and planters she watched Dranit and the man talk for a few moments. Dranit handed the man even more paper bills and the man quickly pocketed the money and scurried away.

She pulled the drapes closed just as Dranit tipped his head back to gaze at her hotel window. She had plunged herself into complete darkness. She groped for the light switch. An overhead light illuminated the room with white shadow-less light. She pressed a hand on the bed. It was a thinly covered affair, as wide as the bed she used to share with Faith before Hope was born. She sought out the attached bath. An indoor toilet, the water wastefully, sinfully, flushing waste down to under the ground. She twisted the knobs in the shower. A grinding noise echoed against the tiles before the water fitfully squirted from the shower head. No replicators, just water. No need for quick showers here, or sponge baths when the water was particularly scarce and the electricity was down.

She cupped her hand under the stream and brought it to her lips. Fresh. If she did nothing else, she planned to stand under this shower and let the water flow. But first, since there was a substantial lock on the door—she would just...

She woke to a pounding at the door.

"Charity?" Dranit's voice was close to panic.

Charity rubbed her eyes. She was fully dressed—she hadn't even removed her shoes.

Morning? Who was knocking? She tried to clear her head. Her body was stiff as she gradually swung her legs off the hard bed. She felt like she had been smacked around with one of those cricket bats she had once seen on TV.

"Okay!" She called out. Dranit stopped pounding.

She carefully opened the door.

"Are you ready for dinner?" Dranit seemed to calm down as soon as he saw her. He had changed into a dark suit with a matching vest, a pale pink shirt and blue and purple striped tie completed his ensemble. He looked like a business man, the kind who did nothing but carry a brief case out of the house in the morning, and then returned with the same brief-case in the afternoon. Mister Cleaver.

She smoothed her hair, at a disadvantage in that she had just slept in her clothes.

"Sleep well?" He grinned, but didn't seem to be insulting her.

"Can I use that bathroom before we leave again?"

"Of course." He glanced behind her into the room and apparently was satisfied. "I'll meet you in the office, which is also the grand lobby."

She looked longingly at the shower, but didn't dare keep Dranit waiting. She settled for washing her hands and face under the warm flow.

Her outfit wasn't right for here. She was too obvious. She noticed a few people giving her a second look, and second looks were dangerous. She needed an outfit that was more in keeping with the city. She considered asking Dranit for help but she sensed that men, whether in the past or the future, did not know that much about women's fashion. Come to think of it, neither did she. She tried to recall if there had been any mention of women's fashion during the history lessons in school, but came up blank. Compared to religion and war, domestic history was not important. She tried to remember photos from the Great Convergence, but try as she could, nothing came to mind. That was odd, weren't there photos? It seemed like there should be.

She braided her hair into a long pony tail and wrapped it around her head and adjusted the money belt so it didn't show under her skirt. It was as good as she could manage right now.

"You must have slept pretty hard," Dranit said as she walked through the swinging glass door.

"Yes, thank you for being so kind."

The man at the counter snorted, but quickly quieted with a look from the other man.

"I am very kind. Let's go get some dinner."

They didn't talk much on the way to the restaurant. Charity

was still taking it all in. They rode past dozens of shops displaying all sorts of things, from dishes to bedspreads to elaborately carved tables and chairs. All claimed quick turn around: Fastest Fabers in Town! No Waiting. Quality Programs. Programs on Account. No Limits!

She passed by a store displaying books for decoration—any title you wanted. She recognized the Dickens and the Sommer, she wondered if they had the third novel in the *Sommer Madison Flats trilogy*.

"Books as decoration, it's the newest trend," Dranit explained. "My grandfather actually has the real stuff." Dranit shook his head. "Crazy, why not just watch the video?"

Chapter Fifteen

The restaurant was located at the top of an old ravaged hotel that itself was perched on a hill so high she feared the car would slip backwards each time it slowed. But they gained the top of the hill in record time, weaving through bands of people dressed in tall hats and feathered headdresses.

"They're calling it the biggest party of the century." Dranit gestured to the noise and crowd outside the car window.

"I'm not sure if it's a riot or a celebration," he mused. "My grandfather doesn't approve, he says that the new convergence will help control this kind of chaos."

"It will," Charity said immediately, then instantly regretted it.

He glanced at her, eye brows raised.

"I mean, it should right? One big organization, everyone equal and, cared for," she faltered. Were they cared for? The men disappeared every day to the Reality Cloud leaving the women to manage with dwindling resources. She turned away from Dranit and focused on the people dancing and singing outside. Most seemed involved in drinking from bottles or enormous red cups. Every block or so, she saw couples locked in a tight embrace, frantically pounding against each other. Men against men, women against women, men and women.

He followed her gaze. "Yeah, there's a lot of sex. It will get worse before Saturday. Once the religions unite, I imagine this kind of display won't be much tolerated." He grinned. "Still for a few seconds, it's not bad."

"Only a few seconds?" She turned back to the couples. A woman submitted to her husband, that was how you made a family. The women here on the street didn't look all that submissive. No wonder order was called for. No wonder the Knight Family and Knight Industries needed to take over. This was madness.

The car brought them to a relatively clear area before the tall hotel. She could see that under the grime, the building was once magnificent.

Dranit took her arm. "I know, it was once the place to be. But the restaurant is still pretty good, and they know me." He escorted her through the lobby. Sunlight streamed through high glass windows and reflected off the tall marble columns. They walked across the marble floor to a small elevator.

As soon as the elevator doors opened, Dranit was greeted like an old friend. The couple was shown to a table overlooking the whole city. Charity couldn't take her eyes off the scene before her. Jumbled city buildings overshadowed tiny people and autocars. Gray-green water circled the piers and lapped at buildings set so close to the edge of land that water reached to second-story windows. *Ah, the Climate Change, all those cars melted the Polar ice caps. At least that part of history was correct.*

The waiter and Dranit began discussing the menus for both the meal and the wine, neither of which Charity had much experience with. She guessed this was part of the dating ritual of the old days—the man takes the woman out, impresses her with his hunting abilities—abilities which were now reduced to knowledgeable conversations with a waiter. But the man still delivered the food—proving he can provide.

She shook her head and sipped the white wine that Dranit assured her was not replicated, but the original thing.

They dined on bright green broccoli florets and chicken so moist Charity didn't need to hack it to pieces with her knife.

Dranit swirled his wine, bright yellow in the stemmed glass. "So, what do you do for fun in your part of the world?"

Watch TV and go to Temple, watch TV after Temple, watch Temple on TV. She smiled brightly and took another bite of food to give her time to compose the answer.

"Oh the usual, this and that." She sipped the wine, not as good as she hoped, but she drank it anyway, to be polite.

"This and that." He leaned forward. "An attractive girl like you? Of age? Okay, then what do you want to do?" His smile spread from his lips all the way to his eyes. "Besides this and that."

He assessed her like he was inspecting the contours of an apple from a replicator.

"I'd like to go to school," she started.

He nodded. "University, great idea. You could go into business. Work for Knight Industries."

Her wine went down the wrong pipe. "Only men work for Knight Industries," she coughed.

"That's ridiculous. We need women—increases the overall intelligence of the group, everyone knows that."

"Really?"

Between the moist chicken and the unlimited shower water, Charity was halfway to declaring herself a permanent resident of this century. Was she that easy? Had Mirabella taken one bite of what Dranit assured her was Dirt Food (he did not use that term of course) and decided to spend her life here?

"Really. But you didn't answer my questions, are you just visiting here or are you planning to stay?"

"What would I do?" She avoided directly answering his question, although she couldn't say exactly why.

He shrugged. "Anything you want?"

Not for long. She forestalled her comment and took another sip of wine, hoping she'd like the third attempt better than the first. She was not successful. She drained the glass anyway. The wine warmed her and made her relax. And for a few seconds she forgot everything except the boy before her.

"What if I want you?" she asked.

He looked startled. "That's not in the cards."

The waiter approached and placed a bowl of red berries before her.

"Strawberries, fresh from the valley," the waiter announced and retreated.

"Strawberries." She examined the fruit.

"Here," Dranit took one of his berries and offered it to her. "Just take a bite, they are delicious, and very rare."

She opened her mouth and allowed him to insert the berry between her lips. It was burst of sweetness she had never experienced.

He watched her reaction and smiled. "Yeah, good huh?"

"Delicious, I've never tasted anything like it."

"Hard to get. We've been using replicators more and more. It's difficult to find fresh food."

She took another strawberry from her bowl and bit in to it. It was unworldly. What else was there to try in this time?

"What did you mean about cards?" She swallowed and picked up another berry.

"You know, tarot, fortune telling."

"The dark arts." She shook her head. "We cannot traffic in those."

"Not interested in learning what the future has in store?"

She smiled and toasted him with her empty glass. "Oh, I'm good for now."

He poured her more wine and she didn't protest.

If she fixed whatever was wrong in this time, what would she return to find in the next? What did she want? Was it the Convergence? Prevent the riots? Or could she just find a way to make her father an executive in the company? Put in a good word to the Knight family.

She regarded Dranit. That may be the simplest thing to do. Just use him.

"Yes?"

"So, what do you do for Knight Industries?"

"You wouldn't believe me if I told you. Let's just say I'm a personal assistant for my grandfather."

"And your father?" she asked. His expression darkened. He took another drink of wine and didn't answer.

"I don't have my family here either." She had no one, except this man who picked her up from the bar like a stray cat. "I apologize, I didn't mean to offend you, it's just that, I am so tired from my travels, you understand how that is." She cleverly appealed to his protective side. Although she wasn't practiced of course, but the suggestion seemed to work.

"Of course." He puffed up his chest. "Travel is very tiring. I'll escort you back to your room."

She tripped on a stair tread leading to her hotel room. Dranit caught her elbow and steadied her.

"The wine must have made me dizzy," she said.

"You get used to it." He guided her to her room and helped her unlock the door, but he did not let her escape into the room.

He stroked her cheek and ran his fingers lightly over her braid. She closed her eyes.

He leaned in very close, his breath smelled like strawberries and wine. As his lips met hers, she thought that maybe this was the whole plan, that she'd meet the man, settle down and be happy, just like Mirabella. Once they married, she could influence Dranit to give her father a future position.

"Please, it's too fast." Her voice was breathless, and in a higher octave that she ever spoke in.

"You're a quick learner. Even in the Eighties it would be too fast." He leaned back and admired her. She reached up and cupped her cheeks that were hot to her touch.

"Okay. Breakfast may be too soon. I'll pick you up for an

early lunch—eleven thirty. Rest tomorrow morning."

She nodded and slipped into her room.

"Lock the door," Dranit called out. "Stay safe inside."

She took her promised shower and stayed under the rushing water until her fingers began to prune, something she had only read about before. She admired the effect and reluctantly turned off the shower. Between the heat of the shower and the food in her stomach, she fell into an exhausted sleep.

* * * *

She had left the curtains slightly open and the morning light slanted through and woke her. A bedside clock blinked 7:00. The enormous flat panel television hovered on the wall across from the double bed. It was the biggest and clearly newest, item in the entire room.

"I understand TV." She flipped it on and quickly scrolled through the shows. She recognized some programs and moved on, only pausing at the news feeds. The Convergence was top news. A small man with what she could only describe as an evil glint in his eye talked of the new Muslim world, how their influence, their part in the Convergence would calm and enrich the world.

Charity shook her head, there would be no Muslim, no Jew, no Christian, all their small differences would be absorbed into the One True Word, the One True God. This time the religions of the world would hammer out a plan, not just agree to respect one another—that never worked anyway.

There was one God, most could agree on that, this time the worship, the rules, the conduct would all be the same. And wars would end.

She paused in her scrolling. Every hour was precious and not to be wasted. She already knew what would happen so the news wasn't terribly compelling. She would head out, have a quick adventure before Dranit could stop her.

She didn't pause to consider why that thought even entered her head, but hurried into her grimy clothes. She could only claim she was in costume for so long, she needed an outfit that would blend in.

She flipped off the enormous TV and was immediately plunged into a disconcerting silence. She frowned, silence was a dead give away. Knowing how much electricity she'd be wasting, but doing it anyway, she flipped the TV back on and allowed the noise to rise and fill the room with purpose and commentary. She opened her door a crack and searched the inner courtyard for any signs of movement or life.

She slipped out under the cover of the newscast.

"David, do we have any perspective on this event?" "No country, no civilization has ever attempted such an ambitious agenda: action rather than talk. This is one for the history books, if we had books!" The newscasters laughed.

"Seriously. This is amazing. In light of what has gone before. The wars. The deaths. This will change the course of mankind. Here with a musical tribute to the unification is our own Bob Marley III."

She shut the door on the ensuing cacophony.

The morning was hurt-your-eyes bright. The sky arched over her like a blue canopy, a color she had never seen. Every other step she glanced up, just to be sure the color was still in place. She walked deeper into the neighborhood, away from the hills that held Dranit's family home. No one was scurrying off to morning prayers heads down, arms crossed. Men and women walked with their heads up. Some pulled up metal doors and unlocked their shops. A few children seemed to be walking to school. They marched along, hands free, hailing merchants as they walked. Charity was tempted to follow one little boy, his dark hair gleaming in the unexpected sunlight. He seemed so happy and carefree. But she didn't want to look like a stalker, or call attention to herself.

She finally found a place that advertised buying real gold and selling the replicated versions. The shop was clean and almost bare, a few replicators on stands, a couple of gold coins on display.

"I have a gold coin to exchange for," she searched her memory, did they call it credits? No, Dranit had paid for dinner with bills, money, that's what he called it.

"Money," she said firmly.

"You aren't from around here? Tourist from the east?" The man greeted her.

"Yes." Charity glanced down at her outfit. Her skirt was dirty from the utility closet floor, her blouse needed washing. "I'm here to celebrate The Convergence."

She forestalled any more discussion by holding out one of her gold coins.

The man eyed it and made many heavy sounds, wheezing and rolling his eyes so much so that she thought he was experiencing a fit.

"May I?" He held out a fat hand. She dropped the coin onto his outstretched palm, and waited.

After ten long minutes, he finally declared it was real. He reached into his own pockets and pulled out handfuls of bills.

"Careful where you use them. We're all going on the credit system. I heard some stores don't accept money, just credit. This new government is all hot for it. But give me the cash anytime." He winked at her. She was tempted to count the bills, but thought it best not to insult the man. She stuffed them deep into the skirt pocket.

The fashion house she understood. A few displays offered a mock-up of the latest fashion. Charity handed the woman at the fashion bar her new bills and stepped into the replicator. In a minute she was dressed in heavy leggings, knee high boots and an iridescent tunic with an adjustable neckline. She sighed with relief when she viewed herself.

"Just stroke here," the sales woman instructed, "to alter the temperature requirements."

Charity nodded, intuiting the process. The outfit could be modified to suit most temperature changes, barring a sand or snow storm.

"It's self-cleaning as well. Do you need any more versions?"

Charity shook her head. She did not want to be burdened with luggage—the bulky money was problematic enough.

She surveyed herself critically. "I need to cut my hair."

"It's pretty the way it is," the girl confirmed, her own hair was hacked to the scalp in spots and long and stringy in other spots.

"Do you have any hats?" Maybe a hat would make her feel more comfortable.

But the hats didn't suit her and she finally rejected them.

Charity brushed her hair back and plaited another thick braid.

By the time she emerged from the Fashion House, the street was filled with people. Bicycles jangled and rang, people dashed in between the bikes, the sidewalks held not only pedestrians but tables and chairs connected to the little bistros and taverns interspersed by replicator stores. People brushed by her, knocking her back, pushing her forward. For a girl accustom to the pace and quiet of a walled city, the noise and activity was chaotic and disconcerting.

Charity pushed against the crowd for a few blocks until she finally felt the rhythm of the pedestrians and could adjust her pace, speed up, and soon feel part of the flow, rather than a buffeted stone in a wind storm.

A shop replicating large screen TV monitors played a current events program. Charity paused. The crawl announced that it was Macpeace Wilson. Charity sucked in her breath and gazed at the screen. Every child knew Macpeace Wilson, it was one of the first things you learned in first grade. He spearheaded the Great Convergence and advocated world peace, the great unification of religions, no more competition, the rise of the family.

"One God, one unification, this is the year, this is the time! We will finally have peace, think about it peace with a capital P!" He thundered. Charity couldn't hear his words on the TV, but she didn't have to, she knew them by heart.

Was she here to help make this happen? But the Great Unification was a reality; it didn't need any help or modification. Ah, maybe she was here to make sure it happened. Was there a threat to it? If there was, the names and record of the attempt was lost to history, part of the dark ages. All she knew was the fact of Wilson and his dream.

"I thought he'd be taller," she mumbled.

Women without men hustled along, some carried electronic pads and slim phones like what Dranit had, most just walked, their hands in their tunic pockets, their bare heads glowing in the unexpected sunshine. Men passed them without giving them a second look. These streets seemed unaffected by the carnival or riots, which was a relief.

She walked by shops stuffed with colorful clothing, housewares, books, TVs, electronics and computers. It seemed that things were produced ahead of time so there was no waiting in line for the replicators to create them. But how did the shop owners know what their customers would want? It was a puzzle.

Charity stopped at the bookstore she had passed the night before.

She couldn't resist.

"Oh, of course I have books." The woman behind the sales counter waved to the single shelf. "Do you want books to read or to decorate? The content books are pretty expensive now, but I keep a few for my collectors."

Sleek small replicators gleamed on the table in the center of the store. Charity brushed her hand across the surface of a few leather bound books. "These are beautiful."

"Of course, nothing but the top-of-the-line here. You can get a computer for less of course, at *Best Price* down the street, but I have the exclusive on the Hassablein line."

"I'd like to buy some books," Charity decided. "To read, not to decorate."

"What's your pay account?" The woman typed a few keys on her computer and looked up waiting for Charity to contribute to the exchange.

"I have this money," she pulled out a wad of bills.

"Money is a pain in the ass. You need an account." The woman was not attractive, her face was marred by deep wrinkles and crinkles, just like the old ladies in the home. Charity tried to subtly check to see if she had all her limbs intact.

"Soon everyone will be connected to the Cloud, maybe we won't even need credits or even leave our homes. We can meet in pretty virtual reality gardens. It will be even better when the Reality Cloud goes live. So much happening this year."

A shout distracted them both and they quickly looked outside. Another bombing?

Five uniformed men marched by, forcing the pedestrians to either side of the sidewalk, not pausing, not apologizing. Charity shuddered.

The bookseller. *Monica Knute*, her name tag said, nodded. "It's sometimes wise not to call attention to yourself around the new Guard. They are very," she trailed off searching for the right term and clearly not finding it. "Persistent."

Charity could imagine. The guards passed by without looking into the store. And both women breathed a sigh of relief.

"What do they do?"

"Keep us all fucking safe," the woman said under her breath.

Charity did not wince, which apparently indicated she had passed some kind of test. "Okay, reading," Monica glanced around, dismissing the pretty books and moving to a shelf that held a jumble of thin, thick, ragged books—books Charity recognized, but to see so many in one place!

She took in Charity's new outfit, her long hair and clean face. "You aren't a pilgrim are you? University student?"

"University student." Charity decided.

"Well then," Monica nodded her head to indicate the back room, her curls bobbed in agreement. "The books are over here."

A big clock with a round face and two pointers hovered over the bookcase. Charity kept an eye on the clock while she scanned the bookshelves. She searched in vain for any history books, specifically the current century, but found nothing. She pulled three books almost at random and quickly returned to the cashier.

"Really, I'd like to use my money." She opened her eyes as wide as possible and tried to look innocent.

The woman huffed and fussed, but finally tallied the total by hand, using an old pencil and scrap of paper and grudgingly accepted Charity's money.

"Can I make a suggestion?" Charity ventured.

"Oh sure." The store owner rolled her eyes, but listened anyway.

"The Cloud is just lovely—but don't you think it would be nice to meet with your friends in person, just so you can really see them? Just in case?"

"In case what?"

Charity glanced around the book store where the fabricators out numbered the books. "In case the power fails."

"The power never fails," the older woman sneered. But she wasn't speaking to Charity.

"Thanks for the books." She'd have to work on her delivery.

Chapter Sixteen

Charity quickly reached the hotel. As she paused to catch her breath, she glanced into the office. The only person in the lobby was Bob, who, she suspected, reported her movements to Dranit. Had he noticed she was missing? Had he leaned on her locked door, and hearing the TV assumed she was safely inside? Had he knocked?

The hotel manager raised his head and looked straight at her. She gave him a wan smile, kept her books behind her back, and shrugged as if to say, what are you going to do? She dashed through the courtyard to her room.

She jerked open her room and was greeted with a torrent of late morning information from the blaring TV.

"George Knight, head of Knight Industries, as well as, the burgeoning Religious Reform Party, accused President Evans of having an affair with his longtime secretary. Vice President Vandermere, a known supporter of private industries and market forces, had no comment.

"The President is not fit to act as head of this new world religion we are organizing, it would be best in the private hands of the citizens." George Knight looked tall, even on TV. His grey-flecked hair and patrician nose filmed rather well—and looking good on TV was 95 percent of politics.

"The Vice President was not available for comment. He will, of course, accompany the President to the talks this week," the announcer concluded.

She rubbed her arms because she was suddenly chilled. To the bone. Her tunic warmed. Macpeace Wilson was a prophet, the Great One, and here she was living in the same time, and he was even scheduled to come to this city for the historic unification pledge.

She glanced at her long braid. She had noticed that most girls her age wore their hair short, but she wasn't quite ready to cut it. She pulled at the tunic neck and the fabric responded and revealed the tops of her breasts. She pulled up on the hem and shortened the tunic as well. She regarded the effect in the cracked mirror hanging on the back of the bathroom door.

In the shorter, tighter outfit, her small size wasn't such a liability. She actually looked pretty good, or even better, she looked more like the women on the street.

She was ready just as Dranit knocked. She tucked her books under the mattress and greeted him.

"Ah, the updated version." Dranit was dressed in a dark jacket and powder blue tee shirt. He pushed up the sleeves of the jacket as she locked her door with an old fashioned key.

"Is that good?"

He fingered her long hair braid. "It's fantastic. I mean, you looked nice before, but now you are more," he paused, searching for the right phrase. "Like a teenage dream."

She stopped walking. A shadow from a potted tree fell across his features.

"You know I went out?"

"Pretty obvious from the new outfit."

"You aren't mad?" The risk she took suddenly flooded over her. The one time she had ventured away from home, broke her routine, she ended up a refugee in another time. It would make sense that doing so again would garner similar results. She glanced up at the sky, clearing to a pale blue.

He sighed and took her arm. "I don't know if I can prevent you from doing what you're going to do. Just be careful, and don't talk to strangers—" He trailed off as if there was more to that warning. She could fill it in—don't talk to other men.

Charity glanced at her companion who was decidedly not her brother or father—or husband. Yet, here they were.

He dragged his hand through his thick hair, and helped her into another autocar. "No matter, you're here safe and sound and we are eating Chinese today." He tapped into his phone and the car executed a neat U-turn and sped through the traffic.

"Grant Street—it used to be famous, reason enough. But they're celebrating the Lunar New Year early, worried it may be the last."

The car couldn't even get close to Grant. It bogged down a number of blocks away from the restaurant. Crowds with dark skin, with light skin, with odd-shaped eyes, dark black eyes, brown eyes, all pressed against the car. Charity drew back even though she knew they were protected by the car windows, but it felt like she was being buried alive under people, whirling and pushing and calling to one another.

"We'll walk." Dranit pushed against the door and dragged Charity across the seat into the crowd. He put an arm around her and held her close as they negotiated the crowd.

Firecrackers startled her. Every time she jumped, Dranit squeezed her arm to reassure her. They edged around a space that opened for a dancing dragon. The oversized head and white teeth startled her. Dancers wearing huge rat masks pranced and gestured behind the dragon.

Charity shrank from the noise and the chaos.

* * * *

Dranit looked over her head at the crowd and felt, for the first time, a twinge of regret. Of course this was chaotic, just as his grandfather and Macpeace Wilson predicted. All the more reason to clamp down on the whole thing. It was as if the crowd was determined to prove the men right—chaos does inspire demonstrations and violence—and riots, he must never forget that. But over the years Dranit noticed that chaos also bred energy and creativity. He watched a small child holding a rat head over his own, the mask had extended teeth that were long and pointed.

What would be lost? When they created the three proposed universal days of worship, encompassing all the religions into one over-served holiday, what would be lost?

He shook away those thoughts. He was responsible for one traveler at a time, one girl at a time, that was all. His family did not require him to think. They didn't even expect it.

Dranit pulled her from the crowds on the street into a ramshackle three-story house. They walked up narrow stairs replete with unfamiliar scents.

A Chinese man met them at the top of the stairs and bowed to Dranit who returned the bow.

"Best food in the city." Dranit led her to a table draped with a thick white table cloth.

"So, where'd you get your new outfit?" He passed her small bowls of rice, meat, that bright green broccoli, pieces of pink shrimp swimming in a dark sweet sauce, and odd dumplings filled with chopped meat.

Dranit wielded chopsticks like an expert, but Charity demurred and made do with a fork.

"I just went shopping for clothes." She gestured to her outfit that was uncomfortably tight now that she was eating, but Dranit seemed to appreciate it.

She unconsciously eliminated her book adventure and turned the conversation to Dranit. She quickly discovered that if she asked more questions about Dranit's hobby, the films and TV shows he loved, she could get through most of lunch without revealing much more about herself.

"What do you think the future is like?" he finally asked point-blank.

She lifted her eyes to meet his. Scenes from *Brave New World* flashed through her head, but she pushed them away. "I have no idea. I hope it's always better, don't you think? Like that plot you told me about where the boy travels back in time and influences his own parents, and his life ends up better."

Dranit nodded. "I'd like to think that too."

When they emerged into the street again, the crowd seemed to be gathering force.

"Why are they so—" she trailed off.

"Frantic?" Dranit pushed away a dozen revelers draped in beads and feathers and little else. He led her to another autocar and they climbed in.

"I don't know for sure, but it seems to me they don't think this new One True God will be very much fun. Better party when they can."

They were very right. Charity watched the couples in the shadows. The dancing and drinking spilled from every doorway and the crowds of people began to encroach on the road.

Enormous screens mounted against buildings and suspended over parking lots filled with autocars. The oversized faces of both Hassied Mohamend and Macpeace Wilson loomed up on the TV screen. Charity already knew what they would say, it was one of the famous speeches from the Unification. Questions twelve through thirty-four on the sophomore year qualifying test.

All women would be protected. All women are safer in their homes. All men will gather as one in the Cloud. Women will nurture the family until the boys are ready to work in the Cloud, the girls, in the home.

The car turned and she lost sight of the screen. At a stop sign there was another screen, this one fitted with speakers.

Hassied Mohamed, in booming tones, guaranteed a clear curfew for all citizens to keep the streets safe.

The news feed switched to the newsroom where a blond reporter turned to her co-anchor. "What do you think of some of these demands?"

"Well Sheila," the handsome TV reporter replied. "I wouldn't call them demands. All religions are working hard to make sure they are heard and rules and ceremonies are protected equally. I know that I wouldn't mind being safe at night, and being able to go to work knowing my wife and children are safe in their homes would be a great bonus."

Sheila did not look as sanguine as her co-star. The man nodded briskly.

"On the entertainment front, will TV star Brittany Manchester finally marry co-star Hank Speak? We have the inside scoop on the romance of the century in just fifteen minutes."

The car moved away.

TV and Video stars were different—in every time. Like many girls, Charity had fantasized about being a star, and foolishly once expressed her wish to Mirabella, who quickly disabused her of that hope.

"You? A star? You have to be part of an important family down in Los Angeles or in New York. We live in the outskirts of the Bay Area—we don't have a chance."

"Sometimes the stars come from the middle of the country. Remember Cecelia Parker? She was really good in *Over the Wall*, and she married that guy. That was a good story."

"Her producer," Mirabella confirmed. "Yeah, that was really great, and you notice she wasn't in any more shows after the marriage."

"That's just the way it should be," Charity mimicked.

"Yeah, whatever. You may want to lay off the TV for a while."

Charity looked at her friend, still in the mood to mock. "Then what else is there to do?"

"Something else." Mirabella lifted her arms to embrace the low gray sky, the gloomy afternoon. Charity looked away and focused on the Lewis home, a pretty colonial mansion with tall pillars flanking the front door. It shimmered and for a brief second she though she saw a squat one story house, but then the image righted and she was back gazing at the original house.

"Read?" Charity suggested with a wicked smile.

"Oh, be serious."

Another enormous TV loomed up before the autocar turned. Charity glanced up at the newscasters, still reporting on the TV stars. *Careful Sheila, after the Convergence, you won't have a job.*

Chapter Seventeen

Martin and Clive Kahn were close. Martin remembered how since they were five the two liked to announce they were just like brothers, a saying their shared mother tired of by the time they were five and a half. They were creatures of the lower southern cities, spending their days conquering the dark dank ghettos on the coast. The slums were too wet for proper people as the streets and alleys were often flooded with both water and sewage. No one bothered to pump them out—the sea would just rise and flood again.

Martin and Clive learned a number of things as they grew up: petty theft, breaking and entering, fencing small items to the shops on higher ground. But it was their skill at eliminating inconvenient people that made their career. By the time they reached their twenties, they were so much in demand it was necessary for some former clients to try to forcibly retire Clive and Martin out of circulation even as it was acknowledged that it would be a shame to waste such valuable skills.

Still, Martin heard that many breathed a sigh of relief when the brothers took a lucrative retainer position with one of the most influential and richest families in the state. Their job, their sacred trust if you will, was to keep the family riches intact and defend the family interests from all interlopers. Sometimes that meant protecting the youngest grandchild, sometimes it meant eliminating direct threats, no matter how old, or how pretty.

"I think our boss is kind of like the mafia. I saw movie about the mafia," Clive, taking on the role of manager explained Sunday afternoon.

"You and your old films." Martin, who considered himself the better looking, scoffed.

"What do you know about old tribes?" He drank down his warm beer and wiped his mouth.

"They weren't like a tribe exactly, just a group with so much money and influence that they could kill people and get away with it."

The brothers met at their favorite pub, a relatively dry place in the higher ground of San Fernando. The area had a checkered history, the most recent still available on video. Most of the homes and establishments sported a great deal of shielding and lead in their ceilings rendering any tracking devices moot. No coverage, no calls. It was as private as you could get.

Martin paused from cleaning his new gun, a prize possession. He had saved for years to replicate it.

"So, who do you think it is this time?" Martin gestured to their bartender, Jones, for another round. His brother wasn't finished he was too busy stroking his prized possession. Martin eyed his brother's unfinished beer.

Clive set down the gun. "For the millionth time, I don't know and I don't care, the credits come through every month, and we don't have to work very hard. How much do we need to know?"

"That sounds like the Knight family," Martin guessed. "You know the ones helping organize that convergence thing?"

Martin shuddered at the mention of the name. It wasn't going to be very good for people in their line of work: a central power; the end of violence; perpetual peace. They'd have to find a way to work in this new Reality Cloud, but how? Can you kill in the Cloud? He should look into that—it could mean his job.

"Probably. Do you think the peace is possible?"

"People aren't good at peace." Martin chugged his second beer and regarded his brother.

"So, do you want to go for the big one, like getting the End Boss? We could make the history books."

"If our names are released," Clive said morosely. "The only way to make history is have your name released, and the only way to get your name released, is to be caught."

Martin wrapped the gun in a clean cloth and slid it into his briefcase that carried the gun, a phone and sometimes a sandwich.

"Is that a yes? San Francisco is nice this time of year. I hear the carnival is tremendous."

"Yeah. Finish your beer."

* * * *

Dranit took her hand and led her to the Embarcadero, the breeze whipped up and she rubbed her arms to warm her outfit.

"Where are we going?" She tugged at her hem to lengthen it and give her more protection from the breeze.

"They used to be called raves. Now it's just called the Party, not to be confused with the wild time out on the street, this is different—no one over thirty is allowed; face to face interaction—no avatars allowed."

He led her past long warehouses and finally to an old building with a faded sign with *Aquarium* sketched over the double door entrance.

No one over thirty, like *Logan's Run*.

Dranit knocked on the tall doors as if this was a secret boys club, or the Reality Cloud.

A huge black man swung open the door and nodded to Dranit, who in turned handed over his phone. The man nonchalantly dropped it into a rusting bucket; neither looked too concerned about the instrument's fate.

The man then lifted a hand—held scanner and swiped it over Charity's arms and head.

"They block our home chips down here, can't be too cautious," Dranit explained.

"Of course not."

The entrance doors clanged shut cutting the noise of the grinding sea and amplifying the noise of the Party. The hard beat of music filled her chest and competed with her heartbeat. She swallowed. They walked down metal stairs that clanged and clanked under foot.

Charity's eyes adjusted to the gloom just as they descended into an enormous room, or perhaps it was the main installation of the aquarium. An enormous water tank, murky and covered in unappealing green slime was sunk into the right hand wall. To the left stretched a long wall painted bright yellow, topped by a sky painted an other-worldly blue. Bold brush strokes along the base of the paint looked like wheat stalks. Black strokes in the blue sky could be birds, or just flaking paint.

The floor below was packed with what at first looked like just heads dyed all different colors. Dranit squeezed her arm and she immediately scanned the crowd. How could he recognize anyone in this melee? But he had different skills, different goals. Charity watched the whirl of people. She could tell they were in their twenties, all, obviously not at home tending new babies and starting out a new job in the RC or a new household complete with rules and tenants that needed to be followed to the letter.

She wanted to yell out, "Enjoy this; in three days it will be all over!" Should she? Would that make a difference? Who would hear? She wracked her brain and tried to recall if there were any rebellions against the Unification. Then again, why would the losers get any mention in the winning history?

"It's a Van Gogh. He was famous for a long time, lots of important people owned his work. It's called *Crows in the Field*." Dranit had to pull her close and yell into her ear to be heard.

"Very colorful."

"Yeah, lucky someone remembered the yellow." He pointed to the far wall painted with a large red arrow.

"There are the toilets. I'll get you a drink. Do you want to try a needle too?"

She shook her head. He shrugged and threaded his way through the crowd that seemed to be fed from a number of hidden entrances.

Her own blond hair seemed rather ordinary. She wasn't even dressed for this. She pulled her neckline lower as she watched a girl in a black net skirt and towering heels stagger against her date, a black-haired boy wearing dark eyeliner and black nail polish. Charity moved a few steps to give the couple room. The girl glanced at Charity, shrugged and carried on.

Dranit had disappeared into the crowd. Charity felt like the final contestant in a reality show—what would happen next? Should she run? Should she stay?

She scanned the crowd searching for Dranit's dark head. She could move around if she wanted, no one was stopping her. Except she was pretty obvious down here, easy to find. She threaded her way to the red arrow.

A group of girls had queued up for the toilets. Charity glanced through one of the stalls. The facilities were little more than holes in the ground with boards balanced on top.

On the opposite wall, five young women leaned over another board and primped before a mottled mirror.

Two girls handed out long thin black needles in exchange for coins. Charity tried not to stare as one girl took the needle and casually plunged it into the underside of her white arm. Her veins stood out like purple lines against her bright white skin.

"Do that too much and you won't be able to sell your organs," her friend chided her.

"Maybe I want to keep my kidney and all of my liver." The girl didn't look at her friend, but concentrated on the needle. "There are other ways of making some cash."

The girl with the needles merely smirked and handed out three more.

"You won't even be able to have babies. I hear the white ones are going up."

"Naw, don't want babies either."

"How did you stop that?"

"I know a woman."

The girls laughed and dodged around Charity and plunged into the melee just outside of the door.

"Don't bother," one of the two remaining girls announced. "They won't listen."

Charity stepped farther into the room. She hadn't noticed, but the two remaining girls did not look exactly the same as the ones who had just left.

The other girl smirked. "We learned fast." She glanced with disdain at Charity. "You, however, look like you're pretty slow, why'd they pick you?"

"Why..." Charity's mind was spinning.

"It's the hair. You need to cut your hair," suggested the other girl. She was dressed in a long bustier, the kind Charity had read about in novels of the nineteenth century, but this one was decorated with sequins and glittered in the low light. Both girls wore fishnet stockings and platform shoes. They looked like every other woman in the main dance hall.

"What do you mean, don't bother?"

The dark-haired girl rolled her eyes, her spangled eyelashes breaking against her charcoal eye brows. "Even if you tell them the truth, they don't listen. No wonder it's so hard to change anything."

"Hannah did." The other girl's breasts pressed against the thin fabric of a stretchy turquoise top. Glitter was scattered over her chest and protruding collar bones. Her hair was swept up in a high hive of hair colored purple and festooned with yellow and blue feathers.

"Vandermere is Vice President—that was a coup."

"She just helped her family."

Charity reeled. "Honesty?"

The girl smirked. "Good guess, at least your brain didn't get too muddled."

"How did you get here?" Charity asked. *When did they arrive? Did they need to return before her? Would there be enough power to handle the return of all three of them? Were they returning?*

"Ditching our pickups."

"Your what?"

"One True *God*, how did you survive so far?" Mary, it had to be Mary, pulled out a lipstick case and began smoothing dark purple color over her lips. "I cannot get enough of this stuff."

Honesty let out a breath of air, but before she could say more, another group of women strolled in pulling out long black needles and laughing, plunging the evil-looking implements deep into their arms.

The music pounded against the swinging door as if trying to enter and invade the impromptu meeting in the toilet. Charity tried not to stare, but every one of the three girls sported long scars on their inside of their arms.

She shuddered but the girls hardly noticed her. They primped, glanced pityingly at Charity's flat, unadorned boots and flounced out.

A headache pressed against her eyes, as if she had seen too much.

Mary waited for the girls to file out then turned on Charity. "Look, I'll help you this one time—you need to get away from whomever brought you here because his only job is to stop you."

"Stop me from what?" Charity's head was swimming from the noise, the smoke, the girls with the needles, the strange scents of perfume (banned in 2060 because of allergies).

"Look, I don't know your family and I don't know what they told you to do. All I know is I need to change my family's fortune, just like Hannah, and live here much more happily ever after than I could hope to live in our time. So you, do not screw us up."

Screw, like the Duck and Screw? Charity just nodded.

"If you do want to help your family, you certainly won't

with your damn baby-sitter out there. You want to do something 'great,'" she contorted her fingers into quote marks, "then you're on your own. This is too big for us to change, so we're out of here."

Honesty leaned around Mary and handed Charity a Bustier and a small can. "Here, at least you can blend in."

"Really?" Mary almost snatched it back from her friend, then just abruptly, changed her mind. "Oh hell, who knows what will change what?"

Charity took the top. It was covered with the same bright spangles as Mary's and weighed at least a few kilos. "This is supposed to make me less conspicuous?"

"You're supposed to blend in," the girl emphasized. Charity longed to quiz them on their own adventure. Did they receive actual instructions? Did they come together? How did they manage that? But she did not want to push her luck.

"Try it," Honesty encouraged. Embarrassed, but realizing they may know far more than she, Charity pulled off her tunic and the compression tee shirt that she couldn't give up before, but apparently was giving up tonight, and laced herself into the skimpy top. Now instead of her breasts being comfortably compressed, they were displayed like hors d'oeuvres. Charity blushed when she saw her reflection in the grimy mirror.

"I don't have scissors," Honesty started, examining Charity's long braid.

"I have a knife," Mary volunteered. She pulled out a wicket switch blade from a tiny silk purse.

"Put that away, I told you, one death is not going to make a difference." Honesty didn't even look up at her friend. She wound Charity's hair like a crown around her head. She shrugged as if that was the best she could do.

"Those eyebrows, very sincere," Mary commented.

Honesty nodded. "I have my tweezers."

"Perfect." It was a toss up as to what looked more dangerous, Mary's knife or Honesty's tweezers. She immediately attacked Charity's virgin brows. Tears streamed down Charity's cheeks as the girls denuded her face.

"Now. Mascara." Mary reluctantly mopped up Charity's cheeks and under Honesty's instructions, painted her eyes with colorful eyeliner and three tones of eye shadow. They applied deep black eyeliner and painted her lips brilliant orange. "We'll put all this on temporary, but you really should get some of this done permanently."

Honesty pulled out a small spray can and deftly covered Charity's hair in purple streaks.

"Excellent."

"I don't look like myself at all."

"Well, whoever brought you in, won't find you now." They look a quick photo of her.

Charity glanced at their phones. "How did you get those past the guard?"

They both shrugged. "Cash is surprisingly effective."

Charity sensed that now their good deed was complete, they would leave her to fend for herself. She tried to delay. "When do you go back?"

They both smirked. "We aren't. We're staying here forever."

The joke Jacob told her, *I'll have everything because I'm not going back.* How much of everything should she take?

"Good luck with changing the world." They waved cheerfully and exited so quickly Charity wondered if they had been a product of wishful thinking and too many novels.

She shook her head and glanced at the mottled mirror. A stranger certainly looked back.

Three more girls shoved and giggled into the room, struggling for supremacy at the mirror. Charity automatically gave them room. This time none of the three gave her a second look.

Well, that was progress. Charity excused herself and made her way to the restroom door. She pushed it open and regarded the seething mass of people outside. Mary's words rang in her ears. She turned back to the girls. "Can I give you a tip?"

They nodded, not sure, of course, if Charity was qualified to deliver relevant information.

"After the Great Convergence, all the women will be asked to stay home." She rolled her eyes at the scene outside. "Don't."

Their eyes grew huge and they nodded.

Satisfied, Charity pushed back into the crowd searching for Dranit's dark head. The Party's action and noise was escalating. Women danced on a platform precariously balanced on wall brackets. Gloomy green light filtered through the murk in the aquarium coloring everything green. Women and men gyrated to the beat as if they had no bones, twirling their blue hair round and round. Flinging their legs and arms up to the top of the ceiling, completely engrossed in the music, oblivious to their partner.

Smoke pressed up against the low ceiling and was slowing drifting down, filling the room with a dense fog, like the TV pattern after eleven o'clock.

"You look lost," a voice yelled in her ear. *My, this was a talkative group.*

"No," she replied without even looking at the speaker. "I'm just looking for my," she stopped and considered the automatic title she had granted Dranit. Was he her boyfriend? Or was she just one of many of his, what did they call her? A pickup.

When girls like Mirabella came back, was Dranit there to pick them up? And put them where? The blood, the blush, every bit of her drained from her head to her feet. He knew...and his job was to turn her into Mirabella. Make sure she settled down with a nice man; have a family. Be happy in the new time and not make trouble. No effect any change at all—the future was secure in the Knight Industry system. Dranit was charming, but she realized that was just his job.

"For someone," she finished.

"That's what they all say." Charity didn't turn around to look at him—she now wanted to find Dranit for a completely different reason.

She finally spotted him off to the left, gyrating against an exotic redhead, her black lips parted, her eyes locked in his. She wore the same skimpy top as Charity but hers was paired with a tight short skirt and see through leggings. Charity paused for just a second to admire how the girl balanced on her sky-high heels.

"If that's him, Paula will keep him occupied for at least an hour." The boy continued to talk to her despite her lackluster responses.

"Really?" She ducked down to avoid Dranit's gaze as he swept the room once more before continuing his focus on Paula and their dance. Was he stalling? Every hour counted, and this was doing her no good. Not with Honesty and Mary's unhelpful attitude.

"Want to get out of here?" the young man asked.

She turned and looked directly into a pair of bright blue eyes, as blue as that painted sky over the stage.

"Yes," she decided. "I do."

Chapter Eighteen

Even as she put her hand in his, she realized he could very well be another pickup artist, and that she was an easy substitute for Mary or Honesty, or Hannah, didn't matter, as girls, they were all alike. Still, he was the evil unexplored, and Dranit apparently has a reputation.

She followed the boy up and out through a tunnel and stairs she hadn't noticed before.

"The piers." He pulled her along an old walkway made of wood, it rattled under her feet in a very realistic way. The sea air was chilly now. The late afternoon sun cast an amber glow on the surviving buildings lining the waterway. The boy gripped her hard and suddenly slowed down so they kept pace with the crowds of people strolling, dancing and performing skits and plays along the wide walkway. In any other time, Charity would have been acutely conscious of her exposed chest and bright hair, but few members busy along the walkway gave her a second glance.

Had Dranit spent the last twenty-four hours plotting to get rid of her? Did he know she was from the future? He must, Honesty and Mary had said as much—or was he just slowing her down so she couldn't return? And this boy, did he suspect she was from the future?

The boy was dressed more casually than Dranit. He wore the faded Levis that had been popular for hundreds of years and a soft plaid shirt that molded to his upper arms and flat stomach.

He led her across a broad avenue and continued quickly into a narrow collection of streets and shops. The pedestrians fell away, the sounds of the Embarcadero was muffled.

"You walk fast for a girl." He finally stopped in a shadowed alley.

She held up her foot. "Low heels."

He nodded. "Nice." He edged to the end of the alley and glanced up and down the street.

"So, where's your sidekick?"

"What do you mean?" She crossed her arms over her breasts and instinctively hunched over to create a little more warmth.

"I mean," he lowered his voice and pulled her back against the side of the building. A couple walked by, not bothering to glance down the long shadowed alley. The wood was still warm from the day's sun. Charity stayed where she was.

"I mean," he continued. "Lovely girls like you usually have a dark-haired best friend, Kato, Sanchez, you know the funny plain one as a foil to your serious beautiful self. The sidekick."

"I was the sidekick." She thought of Mirabella.

He kept watch on the street. "You don't look the part."

She glanced down at the mounds of her breasts and blushed again. "This isn't my usual outfit."

"It should be, you look bloody fantastic. Where are you staying?"

She pulled out a business card from the hotel and handed it to him.

"Excellent. Let's get your stuff."

She held back even as he tried to pull her along. "Why? Why do we need my stuff? Why are we running? Dranit wasn't threatening me—he doesn't even know I'm gone."

He shrugged. "You looked like you needed rescuing."

What she needed was to return to the Duck and Screw. This adventure was clearly not working out, and she wanted to go home. The only thing she had changed was her outfit.

"My name is Matthew."

"Charity." They awkwardly shook hands. He moved again, tentatively tugging her arm. She finally acquiesced and followed him. They kept to back alleys and side streets but he unerringly climbed to higher ground and headed to the district of her hotel.

The back of the hotels were little more alleys closed in by high walls. Enormous dumpsters lined the rear alleys, for a wild second Charity considered them as excellent hiding places. Dranit would never think of looking for her in there.

Then again, maybe he wasn't looking for her at all. She glanced uneasily at Matthew. Who was the better choice when she had zero information to work with? She almost laughed out loud at the incongruity. Her parents chose Ray as her husband because they knew the family. Ray had distinguished himself in the Reality Cloud and was appointed to the Company Guards, protecting the women from the villagers while the men were working together in the virtual reality warehouses.

And she witnessed how much protection the guards were really offering.

They reached her hotel. Matthew pulled her to the back entrance.

"Do you have your key?"

It was safely in her money belt, but she would need to unlace her corset to get at the belt, an activity best done in private.

"Come back through here. I'll be waiting for you." Before she could acknowledge the instructions, Matthew melted back into the shadows. For all she knew, he was planning on hiding in a dumpster.

Honesty and Mary seemed sincere, at least Honesty was. Still, they weren't going back. Charity couldn't imagine just staying here, what would she do? Who would protect and provide for her? And this Matthew? Why suddenly cull her from the herd?

At least Mirabella managed to marry and produce children. Charity wouldn't even rate a mention in Temple at this pace. Staying here wasn't a good choice regardless.

* * * *

"That was a good one." Martin marched down to the end of the alley and inspected his brother's results.

"Five bull's eyes. Why do you think they call them bull's eyes? Who takes the eyes out of bulls?"

"You think too much." His brother snatched the paper target. "Damn good. I'm ready."

"Good. Let's make this quick. Find the girls, take out the girls, get the money and hole up somewhere until Saturday. I'm running out of downloads, this is perfect timing."

His brother grunted and concealed the weapon. He knew to not complain. This was an easy one—one they'd done before.

They headed towards the bay.

"I get the terrorists taking out both the Jew and the Muslim, but do we have to kill more girls? Nice girls?" Martin patted his gun, sort of concealed under his tailored jacket.

"We don't know that they're nice," his brother explained. "They're a threat. We're supposed to annihilate all threats. Just like in the game."

"I love that game, we should play that tonight."

"We will, after we do our job."

"Do we make it look like an accident?"

Martin paused on the street. "I don't think we need to, do we?"

"Just don't get caught," Clive agreed, repeating another condition of their continued employment.

"Of course not, then we wouldn't be able to play our games."

Clive was relieved that Martin had dropped the idea of killing someone famous so they in turn would become famous. That never did add up for him.

* * * *

Charity dashed up the stairs and quickly opened her room. She tossed the room key on the bed and cinched the money belt tightly against her waist. She gazed at the three books she just purchased. Could she take them? She put her hand on the knob and felt it turn under her hand. She stepped back just as Dranit burst through the door.

"I thought you said we always knock." She was so startled it was the first admonishment that came to mind.

"This is an emergency." His grey eyes were dark, his hair was tousled and he was still breathing hard as if he had run the distance from the club.

"Is he still here?"

"Who?"

"The man from the club." He gestured impatiently. He banged open the bathroom door and ripped open the shower curtain. "Have you lost your mind? You don't just leave a club with any man!"

He dropped down on all fours and peered under the bed.

"I left the bar with you." She edged towards the door.

"I'm bloody trustworthy!" he yelled. "You can't leave with him, you're coming with me."

"I don't want to. I want to leave with Matthew."

"Matthew?" He lunged for her and she quickly pulled away, but now Dranit stood between her and escape.

Future Girls

"That man is bad news. You don't even want to go to the corner store with him."

"You're safer?" she asked, left with no weapons but her words. "You just want me gone, put away, like in a cage."

"Who told you that?"

"My, some girls at the club."

"You shouldn't talk with strangers."

"Make up your mind! You are a stranger, and I do not want to disappear."

"Please, you have no idea what Matthew is all about."

* * * *

Unfortunately Matthew Singh wasn't the only person Dranit didn't trust. He had not liked the tone of his grandfather's voice when he scolded Dranit for not elegantly dispatching Charity into marriage or oblivion, which was the same thing in Dranit's mind, within the customary twenty-four hours. Grandfather had even pulled out the ultimate threat—sending Dranit back. To Grandfather it was the ultimate punishment, to Dranit the threat was merely another quandary.

But Matthew Singh was showing up too often at the Duck and Screw. Dranit didn't trust him, and neither should she.

* * * *

He lunged to grab her. She ducked and smashed her arm on his hand, a surprise instinctual move that went against everything she'd been taught about the superiority and strength of men. The girls at the city gate hadn't been able to fight back. She could change that much about the past.

She kicked Dranit between his legs, remembering Jacob's comment about stuff dangling and Dranit immediately doubled in pain.

"I'll choose my own destiny." Her hand ached and she felt off balance. She jerked open the door and plunged down the stairs, her feet barely keeping up with her headlong speed. She turned away from the lobby and dashed to the back of the hotel garden.

No Matthew. She had taken too long. Momentarily flummoxed, she paused. As soon as she heard the clatter of Dranit's feet on the metal stairs, she turned and ran in the opposite direction from where they had come. She wove down narrow alleys, trying to avoid couples, sleeping drunks, and what Dranit called homeless. She kept working up hill, away from the water. She walked fast, heading to the sounds of more revelers or rioters, didn't matter, she could get lost in the crowd.

More and more laughing groups of people brushed past her. With her crazy hair and outlandish makeup, she fit right in.

The height of the party centered on Union Square. By the time she reached it, she was tired, unaccustomed to all the walking and the steep hills. She had a vague plan to find another hotel. Cash must be good in most businesses, she hoped. As she faced the swirling crowds—people wearing rat masks, a long dragon float, and a parade of men carrying women on their shoulders—she questioned her instincts.

She ducked onto a short street lined with galleries and stores still open for business. The store fronts seemed intact, which was surprising. Didn't riots like this involve property destruction?

What pretty colors. She stopped to ease the stitch in her side and used the opportunity to admire the window display. The word Tarantino glowed in cursive script over the entrance. She drank in the turquoise, pink and red swiped onto the displayed canvasses as if the color could warm her.

"You like?" A woman with unruly gray hair and enormous gold earrings stepped outside to the sidewalk. She stood next to Charity and regarded the painting.

"I wonder if it looks better with the glass between it and you. Come in and tell me if that's true."

"I shouldn't talk—"

"To strangers, of course." The woman took Charity's arm and gently led her into the warmth of the store. "However, I am not a stranger, you recognized me through the painting. I am a friend and my work is our introduction. What is your name?"

"Charity."

"Unusual name, *Bible* belt? Pilgrim? Not in that get-up of course. Lovely work. You must share the name of your stylist. Come and tell me about this painting. What do you think?"

The woman moved Charity farther and father into the back of the store. The ubiquitous TV screen blared updates on the Unification talks and assemblies. Alarmed, Charity tried to pull away, but the woman's grip was like iron even as her voice was low and gentle. She maneuvered Charity through the store, keeping them away from the large front window. They slipped behind a tall counter half-shielded by a screen draped with a white and green patterned quilt. Before she could protest further, Charity heard footsteps from outside.

The woman pulled Charity behind the screen, but Charity could still see a corner of the store window. Dranit peered into the store window, and then ran on. She was somewhat relieved that he was moving about and not mortally wounded.

"Not an art lover," her sudden benefactor said sadly. "Ah, and look what he missed." She regarded Charity. "Naturally you are in danger. There are an awful lot of you. Must be the Convergence."

Charity's eyes grew larger as she regarded the woman before her. The woman abruptly released her arm and Charity absently rubbed it.

"The Convergence was a great thing—no war; we are all at peace."

"Like the Great Leap Forward? Sometimes peace is deceptive." The woman paused, regarding Charity. "Frankly, if you are here, and this," she gestured broadly as if to include the shop, the street and the whole of San Francisco, "is still here. Then nothing has changed. Again." She seemed to consider her options. "So, what is your charge? What are you supposed do?"

"Change." Charity gasped. "How do you know?"

"From the future myself. There are a few of us around. Somehow I can always tell. 2150." She thrust out her hand and Charity took it.

"2145." Charity shook the hand, like a piece of the future, her future.

The woman shook her head. "We just need to get you back, if you want to start over and find another time. That would be great."

"Why don't you do it?" The younger woman frowned. "Is it the limb thing?"

"The limb thing," the older woman confirmed grimly. "Time Cults." She saw that Charity wasn't following. "Sorry. You're running away."

"Dranit Knight." Charity's mind whirled. Why send her here if there is nothing here she can change? Unless the status quo was the goal.

"He doesn't want me to change anything." Charity didn't want to believe the girls in the nightclub, but they were right.

"The Knight family will do anything to keep their power. Stephen Knight is tightly aligned with the Convergence, as well as, the Vice President."

"My sister is marrying a Vandermere," Charity mumbled.

"Then her future will be pretty damn bright won't it?"

Charity shook her head. She wasn't that sure at all. Did Faith want to marry? She never asked.

"What are pickup artists and why does everyone know about them except me?"

The woman glanced at the street and pulled Charity deeper inside to a back room festooned with canvasses and heavy drop cloths. "Pickup artists are often from wealthy families who just want to keep their wealth, now and in the future."

"Do they come from the future?"

The woman, who still hadn't given her name, grinned. "Nope. They just know. My best guess is that some of the women who overshoot leave messages that get passed down from generation to generation. Like knowing all the World Series Scores."

"The what?"

"Never mind. Anyway, they know, and it looks like you were caught by one of the best."

Charity looked up at her current benefactor. "Why is it so dangerous for women?"

"It's always dangerous for women, which is what the Unification claims to solve. Everyone will be safe after the weekend. Even you."

An announcer broke through the TV chatter.

"The authorities found this photo, the last post a woman name Honesty Smith made on her phone. If you see this woman please call the authorities."

Charity stared open-mouthed at the TV screen.

Two newscasters, similar to the ones on the morning report, debated about the dangerous nightclubs, the drugs, the dancing, the sex and now, the murder of two women.

"Young people need to be more cautious and less trusting of their peer group," chastised the male broadcaster. "See? This is why the Great Convergence is such a blessing."

The shopkeeper looked from the screen to Charity and back again.

"Hope you aren't too attached to your look, because you're about to change it again."

"They helped me," she whispered, gently touching her bustier. She turned to the woman. "They were from the future too."

Which meant she was next.

Chapter Nineteen

The woman quietly said, "So, do something." She nodded to the huge TV screen. "Make it worth their sacrifice."

Charity cringed. "I can't...I don't know what to change."

"You may want to start with your hair."

"My what?" But before she could protest, or even ask another question, the woman led her to a tiny bathroom, just like the one in her hotel room. The woman pulled out a wicked-looking pair of scissors and calmly began to hack off Charity's hair before she could protest, or cry out.

"We never cut our hair!"

"Close your eyes." The light grating sound of the scissor's blades sent a chill up her spine, but Charity held still.

"Didn't want you to socialize in the beauty parlor I imagine, that makes sense."

"What?"

"Never mind, something else you can change—encourage beauty rituals, the old bathing ponds, women gathering."

"I thought it was our crowning glory." Charity eyed her new look. Her hair seemed thicker, a full bob, her hair just reaching her chin, thick bangs emphasized her blue eyes.

But before she could really admire the effect, there was more.

"Who told you to preserve your crowning glory?"

"The preachers."

"Of course they did."

The woman put her hand on her ample hip to regard her handiwork. "Very nice, but let's lose the purple—too underground club and that particular association won't help you right now."

Charity shook, her teeth chattered. "Dranit must have killed them for telling me to get away."

"Likely. The Knight family is not famous for their philanthropy or their Christmas hams for the poor. They are not only ruthless, but spectacularly immoral.

"Jesus, what is the world coming to?" The gallery owner narrowed her eyes at her reflection floating over Charity's. "Blue would match your eyes, but that may be too much for your first dye job. You don't look like you're ready to defend blue. Let's make it brunette."

The dye job was sloppy but fast. In a matter of minutes Charity's hair was a deep mahogany. The dark hair brought out the bright blue of her eyes. She stared at the reflection. "I've never used so much water on myself in one day."

"Enjoy it while you can." The older woman walked to her cash register. "Now, you need money, lots of money. We can't have you electronically hooked up..."

"I thought I needed to be online to exist."

"Exactly. To exist, but you my dear, don't want to exist. You don't want to be discovered or found. And if the Knight family is systematically eliminating all you girls, then you need to get the hell out of Dodge."

"I thought this was San Francisco."

"No metaphors in the future?"

The new world was wearing thin. This was supposed to be the best of it. Mirabella had mentioned something about guns and Virginia City and Samuel. Charity mentioned that to her new friend.

"Must have been Mark Twain. She traveled too far and too early—nineteenth century. Lots of things happened of course, but nothing that needed to be fixed. Was she happy? Your friend?"

Charity considered that. Had she been happy? Mirabella didn't seem to be in too much pain and she seemed pleased about her unusual life—except for the smoking. "How did she return?"

"It couldn't have been easy. There weren't a lot of electrical currents in that time. You have to catch it, a hundred hours is the basic limit for an in and out. If you stay and live your life, you can return at the same times as another girl travels out, like an exchange program. It depends on the power surges. Egress and ingress. You started at the bar, so that's where you need to head." She regarded Charity with a grave expression. "If you really want to return."

Charity wrapped her arms tightly around her torso. "I have to go back, and I must do it soon, by day after tomorrow."

The woman nodded. "It's compelling, I don't deny it. But

you won't be able to return if you're dead." The sound of the buzzer echoed through the empty store and made Charity jump.

"Good thing I finished with your cut. Come, meet your new partner. He's from this time so there will be continuity and you'll be able to disappear. Plus he owns a car, thank goodness for small favors."

"Why always a boy?"

"Because," the woman said patiently. "Even in the middle of this great..." She rolled her eyes. "...country, a woman alone is in danger. There is always danger. You need someone who knows the lingo and won't give you up."

She pushed Charity towards the front of the store where a lone figure stood at the windows peering out at the empty street. "Here they come," the man at the windows announced suddenly.

"Shit." The proprietor immediately pushed Charity back into the dark of the store. "Hide under the canvasses. Do... Not...Move."

Charity didn't require a long explanation or even further direction. She burrowed under the canvasses, wondering if the new hair color would come off on the heavy material and leave a trace of where she'd been.

She burrowed all the way to the cement flooring and huddled on the cold floor.

The chimes of the front door rattled and sang frantically as a number of heavy booted footfalls marched into the store.

Charity couldn't risk taking a look. Judging from the heavy footsteps and voices, these men were just as big as the Guards at the entrance, men who as easily rape and kill as they do protect and guard. Charity shrank back against the tarps and paintings and sculptures and tried to make herself as small as she could.

"Looking for a girl?" The proprietor drawled.

"Murderer," a guard corrected. "At the Aquarium. What a mess!"

"I don't traffic in girls, just art."

"Important family, don't want her hurt," the guard mumbled.

"I will keep that in mind."

There was a pause as the heavy boots shuffled, as if there was confusion on who would take the lead out of the store. Finally, silence.

Charity peeked out from her hiding place. It was all clear. "You are so brave!"

"Kids," the other woman snorted. "They have no power, just silly uniforms." She looked onto the empty street, just the presence of the uniformed guards was enough to frighten people off. "Does it always have to end this way?"

Charity nodded. "The guards get worse."

"Yes they do." The gallery owner gripped Charity's arm. "Change something."

"I can't change anything...I don't know how," she said.

"We'll think of something," the man at the window finally spoke. He turned around.

"Matthew!" Charity gasped.

"I told you that you can trust me." He grinned and put out his hand. "At your service."

She took his hand and allowed him to lift her away from the folds of the canvasses.

"Where are we going?" Charity brushed her clothes and tentatively touched her hair. She didn't know what to do with it, but left that trouble for a calmer time.

"Road trip, just like the olden days."

Before she let him lead her out the front door into the deepening twilight, she turned to the woman. "Thank you. I don't even know your name."

"The future will be more interesting if you don't." She hugged Charity and held her for a second longer. "Just trust him. He'll get you back in one piece."

Mathew glanced up and down the street, then gestured to Charity to follow. He led her through another alley now filled with the overflow of revelers, the antics of which Charity was growing accustomed to. She didn't give any one or anything a second look. She just followed—sigh—another man.

A light blue, boxy car chirped on as they approached. "Shouldn't it be a convertible or something?" She recalled the TV shows that did feature cars and they all seemed to have no roofs. The passengers and drivers tore down empty roads with the wind in their hair and the sky arching over them like an infinity dome.

"Only if you want that lovely complexion of yours to burn to a crisp, then peel slowly and painfully from your face in long strips of fried skin." He handed her into the passenger side where she bounced on the soft cushioned seat.

"I didn't know the sun was so strong."

He pulled out from the parking space, slowly negotiating the streets heading south.

"No ozone at all, high waters, melting ice caps, you know the whole shebang. I'm surprised Knight Industries doesn't claim they'll solve climate change through religion, it's supposed to solve everything else."

He had changed into a black T-shirt with short sleeves that emphasized his biceps. Charity averted her eyes from Matthew's body and looked out the window. There was scant to see as they cleared the city. Even in the past there weren't many lights for the suburbs and villages.

"Everyone must be in the city," Charity said.

* * * *

Matthew drove deeper into the flat land. He sensed rather than saw the old crop fields ripped apart for coal mining and fracking. The old suburbs were already falling apart

"What is it like in the future?" he asked.

She took a breath. "It's very quiet and orderly. The Great Unification, or Convergence, solved everything."

"My father calls it the next *Treaty of Versailles.*"

"That's good?"

"It was marvelous, except that agreement triggered World War II."

He smiled. "Dranit isn't the only person who studies ancient history."

The car may have been perfect, but the road was not. Once past the suburbs, Matthew had to slow to a mere twenty kilometers an hour. The road disintegrated with every kilometer. The car dropped into pot holes and sputtered on patches of gravel. Matthew struggled to keep the vehicle on its straight course.

* * * *

Charity was certain that they would blow a tire, or wrench an axle, or whatever you do to independently operated cars. They swept by towns dominated by abandoned gas stations and derelict motels.

"Where are we?"

"The old 101 highway. It leads away from the City. Obviously whoever is after you has already reached San Francisco. We'll wait them out. Once the Great Convergence is signed, sealed and delivered, you'll be out of danger."

"Wait them out!" Charity's stomach clenched with alarm. She counted the days in frantic calculation. "I have two days before I'm stuck here forever." A life spent waiting for the chance to return, trying to figure out the future from an intractable past, "We need to get back! Turn around!"

She lunged for the steering wheel, but Matthew was stronger. He wrapped his hand around her wrist and squeezed until she cried out.

A long train, the same kind as she and Jacob took to San Francisco, shrieked just as she did, drowning her protests. The train, running parallel to the highway, shrieked again and ground to a complete halt. Immediately people poured from the cars like blood from an open wound.

"What happened?" She jerked her hand from his grasp and rubbed her wrist.

"The trains break down all the time." Matthew pressed the gas and they zoomed past the former passengers, searching for their luggage, calling to each other, some screaming questions at the uniformed officials.

"I never heard that."

"The media never says."

He glanced at her again. She nursed her wrist.

"Sorry. I'll get you back if you want. Saturday? That's enough time, we'll return right after the Convergence rituals. By then Knight Industries will have what they want and you won't be a threat."

* * * *

"Who the fuck got the girl out of the city?" Clive demanded. He shut off his phone in disgust.

"We'll catch her. Chance to try out our bikes," Martin consoled his brother. "Like those road trips...easy rider."

"We only have two days." His voice was high, whiney, as if life was unfair.

"Easy, with all the partying in the City, how hard can it be?" Martin stroked his wrist to call up the beta version of the Reality Cloud. Great thing, always having every bit of information a man needed, when he needed. He connected into the private Knight Industries site and searched for the target. Not hard at all. He pushed away the thought that easy Cloud tracking would put them out of business. First things first.

* * * *

Mathew pointed out the old, abandoned universities and towns appearing first as long shadows, then in full as the sun gained the sky.

"Where are we—" Charity began. Just as she started her question, they rolled around a corner, hit a pothole and almost plowed directly into a milling group of men blocking the road.

"What the hell!" Matthew slammed on the brakes and skidded, narrowly missing a man carrying a sign painted with the words Independence. Before they could react, dozens of men quickly surrounded the car. Every other man carried a sign—most decrying joining the church (any church) and state, some protesting Knight Industries. Not one man touched the car, no one tried to climb onto the car. The men stood silently, blocking the road.

Charity regarded the protestors. Were these the grandparents of Jacob and Betsy? Was this how the outliers began?

Matthew squinted through the window trying to see past the press of bodies. "Must be one of the mines."

Something nagged at Charity. She pushed open her door. The men pulled back giving her room, but then closed ranks quickly around her. She nodded and smiled, pushing gently the thin, haggard men out of her path.

Matthew followed. "What are you doing?"

"Something, anything." She wasn't even thinking of her parents or the future. At the very least, these people needed to know this was not the course to take. Theirs was a precarious situation. Now that she saw them in the flesh, she realized that what had been written in history was not the same as what really happened.

The men pulled back revealing one of the most disreputable protesters in the group. With long hair and a thin long beard, he looked awful and a bit frightening. He held a sign demanding minimum wage.

"They will invent a machine," she said under her breath, so that just the man heard her and not his compatriots surrounding them.

"Who are you?" He was tall, but stooped, so they were roughly the same height. She stared into his blue eyes and felt a fissure of recognition. *Which was impossible.*

"The family, the Knights, will invent a machine to extract the shale for much less than they pay you. You will continue to protest, dismantle the machines, blow up part of the mine. It won't work. None of it will work. You will still lose your jobs." Now she could see the pit mine with a row of tiny homes skirting the edge. "Your whole way of life."

The man snorted. "Listen missy, we know what we're doing. They can't get the stuff out without us. So, we want more."

She nodded. "What town is this?"

"Morgan Hill."

There had been a massive village uprising here. Not this year, she couldn't remember the exact date, but there had been TV shows about it. The docudramas had depicted evil villagers pitted against the virtuous Knight Industries—who, in the end, only wanted to make sure that no matter what, the people would get their electricity to run the Reality Cloud. The show ended with dramatic annihilation of the entire town. Just because the Knight family had invested in mining, didn't mean they did not have access to nuclear weapons. She remembered her father mentioning that this area of the country had been off limits since the time of the Great Convergence. Not even old airplanes few over the wasteland.

She winced at the recollection. The man mistook her body language as a reaction to his tone.

"No offense miss, but I think we know what we are doing."

"If I told you this was futile—that you would all die because of the strike, would you believe me?"

He waved his sign. "Of course not."

She nodded and headed back to the car. But she could not leave it like this. She turned back and cupped her hands around her mouth. "Why are you doing this with only half your people?" she shouted.

The men froze and looked at her as if she had grown snakes from her head. She smiled and waved. "Good luck!" Matthew opened the car door and she slipped into the seat. "They're going to need it."

"Help?"

She shook her head. "Not at all. Damn, even when I blurt out the truth, no one wants to hear it."

"The curse of Cassandra," he acknowledged. "You can tell us everything, but all we really want to hear is what we already know."

"Sounds like the news."

Chapter Twenty

"Only a little farther." Matthew pulled into an old gas station. One pump seemed to be operational while the rest looked rusted and grimy.

"Then where?" She had asked that question many times, in as many ways as she could think of even as the sun arched over head, then began to slide away to their right, leaving her with very few hours to squander. But Matthew was less interested in assuring her and far more interested in her life, which, when she explained it out loud, only took a few minutes.

"What about the Reality Cloud, how do you get in? How do you win?"

"I don't know," she admitted. "Girls aren't allowed, just boys."

He frowned, but she wasn't sure if he was upset with her, or upset with society. She hoped the latter.

"Hello?" Matthew called out as he exited the car.

Up the hills glinted brand new shining copper pipes, suspended a foot above ground—faster to lay, easier to repair. Her memory of the rotted, pitted pipes leaking sand and chips of rust overlaid the new promise that stretched out before her.

Charity studied the wires from generators laid around the gas station. A wind mill squeaked overhead, a small stove belched out noxious black smoke.

"Welcome." A man, his face creased and tan from the relentless sun came in from a barn behind the house. "Cold water over there; toilet in the back."

"Thank you." Mathew walked to the toilet first.

"You look well set up here," Charity said.

"We're almost completely self-sufficient," the man agreed. "Of course, coal is the best source of energy."

Charity didn't disabuse her host.

"Love what you've done to the place." Matthew emerged from the toilet. "Kind of like Mad Max meets Laura Ashley."

"The flowers were my wife's idea." He pointed out a generator humming away under a chintz cozy.

With a sudden flash, Charity realized that she had been talking to the wrong people. She wasn't going to convince any father that his choices and beliefs were wrong. He had too much at stake to be corrected. To be wrong was to risk his family and his reputation for nothing. Every back to the land farmer who had wrenched his children and wife from the city because he believed in a different life, had to be right about that life. He was *the father*. In any time, in any country, he had to be right, because unlike her, they could not go back.

"Where are your children?" she asked.

"Out in the field."

She nodded to the father and headed out to the barren rocky fields. "I won't be long."

Two boys, about twelve or thirteen years old, hoed the recalcitrant land. Their smaller sister pulled the rocks from the soil and stacked them along the edge of the field.

"Hello," Charity struggled over the rocky soil rock soil. "I'm Charity, just visiting. What are your plans out here?"

The boys paused. One of them said, "We'll make a go of it. Be on our own. Once we get all this up and going, we can tell Knight Industries to go to hell."

"Water?" Charity asked reasonably. She heard the sound of another engine, probably a car, whoosh past, but she didn't see anything.

Since she was a child, Charity had listened to the stories of wars, famine, riots and religious unrest. If it wasn't for the great unification at the center of San Francisco, all would have been lost. And if it wasn't for the Knight family saving all the Unification delegates from the earthquake, a grateful city and state and finally the world, would not have offered them the ultimate prize—control of the Reality Cloud. Without Knight Industries, there would be no replicators to provide for their every need. They wouldn't have food or decent water.

The One True God, the Company and the Reality Cloud were the three cornerstones of their good life here in California. It's what held them all together.

Only the rebels left the comfort and safety of the suburban cities after the Great Unification. Anyone who disagreed was repurposed, it was the only way.

She studied the words. She listened to the logic. She had scored one hundred percent on the test. She reasoned that she should know.

"We'll get water from the Government, after the Unification. They have to send it. We're the raw source for the food pods and replicators," the boy patiently repeated the family mantra, their reason for existence as his brother grinned. "So the water will always come." He pointed to the shiny new pipes parallel to the highway.

There was a better way, but they would need to do it now, before they were completely dependent on the government, and soon, Knight Industries for water, power, everything. It was only a matter of time before corn would become the dominate crop used as the base for all the replicator pods. The other dirt foods would fall off, as would the families who tried to compete with Knight Industries.

"You are familiar with solar panels?" she asked.

"Yeah, Dad has a few old ones in the barn."

"You may want to work on those too"

Mathew rose over the horizon waving his arms.

"I have to go. Solar panels. Make your own electricity. It will help you later."

She patted the boy's back. "Also, dig a well." She scrambled up the bank and joined Matthew.

"I spotted some motorcycles, we need to go."

"What's wrong with motorcycles?"

"Nothing." He scanned the horizon, narrowing his eyes. "Perfectly innocent. That's why we need to go."

She didn't question, besides, he was driving.

It wasn't until dusk that she spotted the copper mine—the green tailings glowed in the sunset. If the mining wasn't so obviously devastating, it would be beautiful.

"Copper." Mathew slowed, but didn't stop.

"Slow work." She watched men pick and dig and manipulate small hand-cranked equipment to dig out the ore.

The work was being done slowly, but was being done.

"Who controls the copper mines?" she asked idly, not really expecting Matthew to answer.

"This..." He stepped on the gas. "Belongs to my family. Although I don't know why we keep the mines open; can't use copper for anything."

She nodded. "Phones run on copper wire. Direct, only a little electricity needed."

"So? We have implants now...always on, always working." He gestured to his head. "Unless of course, you get them removed."

"Exactly—and if there is no electricity? Then how would you reach people?" She scanned the low hills that looked denuded of everything. In the distance taller mountains began to climb into the sky.

"You are smarter than you let on. In the future are there books, newspapers, hard copy?"

She turned away—of course there were books: banned, secreted, carefully preserved and exchanged. The last place to find information.

"No. No books. We get all our information electronically," and since he was so keen to learn about the Cloud, "all through the Reality Cloud."

The sky darkened around them, but Mathew made no gesture to slowing, and she didn't bring it up yet. The tires alternately hummed, skidded and bounced. They passed trucks hauling five and six containers each, filled, Mathew told her, with food pods for replicators. They whooshed by the Volvo and rumbled away to San Francisco.

"Tomorrow is the Convergence." Charity didn't know if it was safer here, away from the City or if she should take her chances. She needed to get back. She drummed her fingers on the arm rest and shifted, unable to get comfortable. She wanted to ask again where they were going and why. This was the wrong way, she was sure of it.

"Tell me more about the future," Matthew broke the silence.

"Are you sure you want to know? You've witnessed my success rate."

"Yeah, but I'm not a farmer."

"No, no you aren't." She studied him. He was handsome in a rugged way. Those blue eyes were compelling of course. His face was long, very much like...no, that was too much of a coincidence. She covered her confusion by talking about what he probably wanted to hear.

"You already know about the dark ages. I think this century counts as well, but we don't know much about the Twenty-First Century."

Mathew shot her a look. "What do you mean? There's no information about this century?"

"The electronics were all erased, deleted. All electricity is channeled to the Reality Cloud...there's only a small amount for domestic use."

It was a simple explanation, and she had accepted it for as long as she had been alive. There was no real history. What was important was the here and now. They were safe, happy and they had the *New Bible* and the One True God. That was enough. Then why was she here?

"Fuck me dead," Matthew muttered. "They wiped it all out. Wiped out the controversy, wiped out the—"

"Controversy?" Charity interrupted him. "There was controversy?"

Chapter Twenty-One

"I know a place where we'll be safe."

"I need to get back!"

He paused and jerked the *Volvo* off the patched highway and onto an indifferently tended gravel road. The car bumped and shuddered.

"We can help you." Matthew kept his eyes on the road. "My uncle has abundant resources. We need to keep you away from those yahoos following us."

"Followed?" Charity twisted and tried to look behind her, but all she saw was dust. "Aren't you leaving a trail?"

"Once we're with my uncle, they can't touch us—you."

"You seemed prepared," she hoped for more clarification, an outline of his plan, but he was not forthcoming.

"Boy scout marching song, baby." He grinned.

The car bottomed out. Charity clutched at the dashboard.

"Shit, there they are." Matthew glanced at his arm, grimaced and pressed on the gas.

"Can you outrun motorcycles?"

He glanced in the rearview mirror. "Not really."

"What?" She looked out the dusty back window. Two motorcycles rose over a hill and revved their engines. The noise was deafening and decidedly menacing. "They don't look—" a huge explosion interrupted her. A crater opened right in front of the car. Dirt and rocks rained down on the roof. Matthew jerked the steering wheel and ran the car off the gravel road and hit the pockmarked desert.

* * * *

The motorcycles followed. One of the riders tossed another explosive to block their way again. Shots peppered the car.

"You're supposed to throw the grenade at the car you idiot," Clive yelled at his brother.

Martin pulled off the cumbersome helmet that had been itching him for the last 128 Kilometers.

"I can't see a fucking thing with this on." He threw the helmet behind him. *Take that Safety Class 102.*

He pulled out another grenade and pulled the pin using his teeth, mostly because he thought it made him look more dangerous. Like his favorite hero in *Road Rage IV*, he threw the grenade at the car, but it swerved again and the grenade blew up nothing but dry dust and sand.

"Bloody hell." The sand flew into Martin's unprotected eyes.

"Shouldn't have ditched the helmet!" his brother yelled and laughed.

"You try hitting a moving target," he yelled back, rubbing his eyes with one hand while negotiating the motor bike with the other.

* * * *

"What are they doing?" Charity pushed her head and shoulders out the passenger window and tried to find their pursuers through the dust, sand and fading light.

"In," Matthew roughly pulled her back into the car with one hand. "Don't give them a better target."

"What can we do?" She watched anxiously in the side view mirror.

"They aren't after me," he said brightly. "Must have figured you out. From the looks of it, they sent a couple of their hired boys."

She slumped down. "How much further?"

"We're really close." He focused on the rearview mirror. "Here they come. We may need to make a run for it."

"Wha—" But, before the word was out of her mouth, Matthew jammed the car next to a boulder. Bullets kicked up dust and stones that hit the car like a second assault wave. Bullets hit the back of the car and shattered the back windshield.

He pulled her out of his side of the car to get more of the car between them and the rain of bullets. But it wouldn't take much for the men to circle and attack from their open side.

More bullets pock-marked the car. Matthew winced. The car held and absorbed most of the bullets, but probably not for long.

"Jesus."

"At one with God," she automatically responded.

"That's nice, but what are we going to do?" He ducked as another bullet whizzed by.

She surveyed the bare ground behind them. The bullets were fewer, but more strategically placed. She ducked as one pinged close to her ear.

"See that bunker?" She gestured to what looked like a pile of dirt and debris.

"What bunker?" Mathew squinted against the creeping gloom and focused on where she pointed.

She glanced around the open car door. "How do we get them to blow up the car?"

He looked at her in surprise, then her plan dawned on him. He nodded.

"Fuckers! You will never get us!" Matthew yelled.

She screamed something along the lines of "You can't take me," although she wasn't all that clear, didn't matter, it was the noise that mattered. She grabbed Matthew's hand and pulled him along the rough ground to the unassuming mound. She violently and desperately dug away at the base of the mound, found the entrance and dragged Matthew behind her into the dark.

The familiar smell of damp earth assaulted Charity's nose. She wasn't over her fear of the earth pressing down on her. She swallowed and steeled herself. *No hysterics, breathe.* She was grateful for Mathew's presence, another warm body in hiding made all the difference.

"What—" he began.

"Shhhh."

Charity heard a man's voice from a few meters away say, "Really?"

"Blow them up?" came the other voice.

Charity listened for more discussion, but it seemed to be just the two.

"Hell yes. We need to get going."

"I loved that car," Mathew whispered.

"Shhh." She rustled around and pulled up some branches to stuff into the opening, plunging them into complete darkness.

They waited, barely breathing.

Then it came, an enormous explosion that rattled the dirt down on them.

"Yeah!" a voice bellowed. "Take *that* mother fucker."

"Do we come up with anything more original in the future?" Mathew whispered.

"We are fined if we swear," she whispered back.

She felt rather than saw him nod.

The fire roared, then quickly died. She felt Mathew shift his weight as if to poke his head from the bunker and look around. She grabbed his arm and held him back.

"No, that's what they will look for. Stay."

"How do you know?"

"Done this before."

Charity at first heard the two men mumble as they as they circled the still-burning wreckage of the car. Their voices came clear again as they neared where she and Matthew hid.

"I think that last one did it. I threw that last one. Did you see it?"

"Just like level six in *Warp Speed*. The boss will be very pleased. Hey, let's take a few photos to show him. Pity there aren't any charred bodies or pieces of clothing."

"Can't have everything. Come on, we gotta go."

After a long pause Charity heard the motorcycles rev up and scream away.

Matthew made another move, but Charity kept her hand on his arm, or maybe his leg—any appendage to stop him from popping out of the bunker like a cartoon gopher searching for his shadow.

"Shhh."

She waited, but didn't hear returning footsteps. Had she thrown the grenade, she would have circled back one more time just to make sure the quarry wasn't hiding in a nearby bunker. But apparently their nemeses were not so inclined.

"Let's just stay undercover for a few more minutes," she suggested.

"I have nothing else to contribute, so fine by me." Matthew shifted and inched closer to her. "Would you like the hard ground or the area over here riddled with pointy stones?"

Chapter Twenty-Two

They spoke in broken desultory sentences. The darkness was close to absolute. Charity could barely see her hand before her face. She felt, rather than saw Matthew.

"World peace," he repeated. "But what goes on in the Reality Cloud?"

"My father says it's just a lot of meetings and discussion, not all that interesting." That was the truth as far as she knew it. Matthew did not seem satisfied.

"You've seen it?"

She remembered telling Mirabella that if girls could do anything in the Reality Cloud that boys did, it would change their whole lives. There were rumors of course, but she didn't feel that she should feed Matthew rumors.

"What did you mean that there was controversy about the Great Unification?" She changed the subject.

"Just that one overreaching religion or government or anything doesn't sit well with some people."

"It's all about the big things," she said. "What about the small things? I have, what, twenty more hours."

He moved closer to her. She felt his warmth and imagined his blue eyes. She reached up and felt his cheek, rough at the end of the day. She slid her hand down to his jaw, to his neck.

"You want to take advantage of all the adventures life can hold?" He slid a hand up her arm, brushing her breast.

She shuddered, not sure if she was repelled or fascinated. She realized that every book she read wasn't really helpful in a real life situation. The phrase, the joke, came back to her—I'll have everything because I'm not going back. Her fingers trailed down his neck and to his chest. She felt him swallow and held her hand over his heart. She felt it pound under her fingers. He groaned and pulled her to him, then rolled quickly over her, thank goodness—she thought with her last real sensible thought—she wasn't on any stones.

His mouth came down on hers and she met it with a vigor

that surprised her. Matthew pushed his hard groin up against her and ground her more deeply into the rough ground.

"Charity."

She pushed him up and braced her arms.

"Come on," he whispered urgently. "What if saying yes changes everything?"

She felt his muscles under her fingers. Her heart beat as rapidly as his, her lips bruised but somehow was ready for more.

"What if saying no does?"

He paused, she could feel his arms tremble. Then with a groan torn from his soul, he pulled away and rolled to the far side of the bunker. "I'm sorry."

Charity pulled her legs in and wrapped her arms around them.

Matthew rose on his hands and knees, breathing hard. To distract himself, he approached the entrance and peeked out between the sticks and rocks. "It's dark enough, and there's no one next to the poor remains of my car."

She climbed out of the bunker on her own while he regarded the final flames licking at the twisted metal of the car.

"Is it far to your uncle's?"

"He's close. I can tell from the stars."

She looked up. The range of stars, the light, the vastness. The sky stretched over them, the stars looking like they were painted white against a brilliant purple and dark blue. Traces of clouds glowed pink in the waning light.

"It's like watching time travel; those suns are dead by the time we see them."

"So we don't see them until it's too late."

Their trudging, shuffling walk in the dark was at least made easier by the road. They hiked as far as they could. Mathew took her hand to steady her and never let it go.

"It's longer on foot."

"Time always slows when you aren't having much fun."

"I'm having fun," he said. "Getting shot at, shepherding a girl from the future to her destiny, aiding to construct my own altered future. Big fun."

She couldn't see his expression in the dark. "Are you teasing me?"

"A little. It helps pass the time."

They walked in silence for half an hour. Finally Matthew

spoke again. "You keep talking about the Villagers, are they the workers?"

"Yes, they live off the grid, outside the Cloud."

"So, they're the rebels." Matthew kicked a rock out of her path. "You know, rebellion doesn't always have to be a big showdown. It can be a small thing, like not giving up your seat on the bus."

"What?"

"Never mind."

They climbed the next hill and Charity caught her breath.

"What is this place?" Before her rose an enormous metal building pushed into the hill side. Surrounding the large building stood a wall of tall vicious stones, sharp and piercing the ground like lightening bolts gone awry.

"A landscape of thorns," Matthew said. "I never get used to it."

"What are they for?"

"A warning, before we figured out how to tap into the depleted uranium. Now my uncle just uses the scary sculptures to keep everyone out."

"Isn't the ground dangerous?"

"Don't worry." He read her expression of horror. "You won't start growing extra limbs right away."

"It seems an odd place to live," she commented. They carefully threaded between the sharp warning stones and approached an enormous metal door that didn't seem to have any handles.

"Not so odd. No one bothers him. He claims that he can get pizza delivered here, but no one believes him."

Matthew banged his fist on an old-fashioned intercom mounted to the left of the door.

"Uncle Hugh, I have someone for you."

"My boy!" bellowed a voice through the intercom. Charity was ridiculously reminded of the scene in the *Wizard of Oz* when Dorothy knocked on the great door to the Emerald City. Dranit would have appreciated the reference. She suddenly missed him, but he was the bad guy. Matthew was the good guy. Right?

The huge doors clicked open. "Go straight ahead and take the first right, you can't miss me."

The two young people slid in. The doors banged behind them. It took Charity a minute or two to adjust to the dim light but at least there was light, as well as, smooth floors and high ceilings. Not underground. She took a deep breath of thanks to the One True God and stepped forward. Mathew walked behind her. They followed both the directions and the noise, a loud throbbing sound that seemed to come from deep within the hill.

The two turned right into the first hallway they found and Charity gasped with amazement. The room seemed to be one huge warehouse filled with hundreds of computers and even more books. The low hum indicated there massive power available to keep everything lit and moving.

"My boy, my boy." Uncle Hugh was a slender man, and the same height as Charity. His thick glasses emphasized his eyes in an odd way. Instant *Lasik* must not be common yet. He hopped over a pile of books and clutched Matthew in a hug. Matthew looked over his uncle's head and winked at Charity.

"You brought me a girl. Welcome my dear. Just a minute."

A Farber dinged and Uncle Hugh scurried over and pulled out a book. He thumbed through the page and nodded.

"How rich, *1984*, and look." He fanned the pages: all blank.

"Those are real books?" Charity reached out a tentative finger and touched the smooth cover.

"Of course they're books, just empty. We're distributing them for decoration. The book look."

The closest pile of books drew her to them. She plucked up one and almost compulsively began reading until she remembered herself. She looked at her host.

"Translating." The spry man gestured to the computers. "Everything we write—all the emails, the e-books, the newspapers, the magazines. From written word to pure data, we will have it all! No need for those." He pointed to the book Charity held. She gripped it compulsively as she considered the project spread before her. An ancient *Espresso Book Machine* ran in the center of the room printing out a single copy of a book. She itched to pick it up and see if she had read it already.

"My job is to copy everything and store it. That way..." Hugh trailed off.

"We have everything, all stored and neat," Matthew confirmed. "We have something to negotiate with when the Cloud goes live later this year."

The machine dinged and Charity lunged to be the first to

pull the finished book from it. The cover was poorly reproduced, and the paper was thin and fragile, even when new. She fanned the pages. The book felt familiar in her hands. These were the pirate copies. These were the books she hid in the hollowed out pages of her *New Bible*. She almost tucked it under her bustier, just because it was such a practiced gesture.

Hugh gently took the book from her and tossed it into a pile.

"Books as decoration," Charity repeated, just to be sure.

"No one reads the books on their shelves anyway." Hugh's expression was kindly. "Isn't that right?"

"They learn everything through TV or the Reality Cloud." Matthew's voice sounded odd to her, but she didn't challenge him. He was her ticket back to San Francisco. She glanced around the solid building. Unless they planned to keep her here. But what was the point?

Hugh gathered a handful of the empty books and plopped them into a box.

"Uncle Hugh was always the cut up, but then he got on the wrong side of the new government. They raided his house and everything. He never told us why." Mathew gathered up handfuls of cash and packaged food and stuffed them into a cloth bag. "Why are you in hiding Uncle Hugh." Matthew concentrated on his task.

"Not telling—bad for you to know."

* * * *

The photo didn't convince the head of Knight Industries.

Dranit shifted uncomfortably in the ancient chair which had all hard angles and no cushion.

"Do you want this to disappear? It does affect you, you know. No more parties, no more living in the City, no more power." The older man shuddered. He set down his phone and admired the photos of the black, smoking Volvo.

"Then send me back." Dranit tensed, he knew it was inevitable, every time he met with his grandfather, he was ready.

"No need. I sent them back to finish the job." He gestured to the projections even as his grandson looked in horror at the twisted metal. Dranit squinted, the image shimmered, he couldn't see anything more than the car, but that could just be the quality of the image.

"I need you to make sure." His grandfather addressed the phone this time

A howl that even Dranit could hear indicated that the brothers were not happy about their sudden job security.

Dranit took in the opulence of his grandfather's office. It wasn't all that risky if you presented the past in the right light. As far as he knew, the girls always chose to stay, that was the goal. Trouble was, no one really knew if she had been successful or not.

A word caught his attention as his grandfather continued to reason with his hired men. He signed off and looked at his grandson.

"You're going to kill her," Dranit said. Then a more horrible truth dawned. "That's what really happened to all those girls, isn't it?"

His grandfather, an elegant man in his fifties, tapped his temple to end the call. "Of course. Don't be naïve."

Dranit rose slowly from the uncomfortable chair. Ice ran through his veins and his head began to throb. "You said they were safe."

"Of course they're safe. You can't get in trouble if you are no long with us."

Those pretty girls, those hopeful girls. All from his time, all reminders of a home he would never see again.

"Why didn't you just kill me?" He gripped the chair arms, his body was cold.

"What? Kill a future grandchild? An eight-year-old? You may not believe it right now, but even I have my limits."

Dranit swayed. "How do you know I won't change things." He gestured to the office, taking in more than just the room—the whole enterprise. "To be different?"

"Ah, but you already have. Moving the Great Convergence ceremony to the coast to avoid the mobs was an invaluable tip. A last minute switch, brilliant! Think of the terrorist and assignation attempts we will thwart!"

His grandfather grinned wolfishly, the expression was disturbingly similar to the face Dranit saw in the mirror each morning.

"You, my boy, have earned your keep twelve times over. You won't go back. You are perfectly suited to stay here. I'll make you a vice president. But..." he leaned forward and regarded his grandson coldly.

"If you really want to get to the girl before my men do, you'd better hurry."

* * * *

Clive hoisted a long barrel to his shoulder and concentrated on the bunker door.

"Is that the P38 DNA splicer—second generation?"

Clive nodded.

"How in the hell did you score a rocket launcher?" his brother demanded, not un-envious.

"Gun show." Clive squinted and released the rocket straight at the door. There was a brief pause as if the door would actually hold against the impact. But in a second, the door shuddered. A split second after that, the explosion rocked the brothers back on their heels.

Clive nodded with satisfaction. "Waiting period was only two days."

* * * *

There was something she had heard from Preacher John, lecture number forty-five: why reading is dangerous. In the twenty-second century all the books burned, something burned, it was part of the dark ages when all the light went out. And of course all the work in the twenty-first century was completely lost. It was if they were all starting from scratch.

"I do know what happens here," she started to say.

An enormous explosion stopped her, she stumbled and Matthew caught her. Charity saw a bright light and flames where Uncle Hugh had stood.

An alarm sounded, shrill and unnerving. Massive sheets of metal began to descend and cut off the exits behind them.

The walls closed in. Matthew pulled Charity along.

She heard sprinklers start up in the hallways.

"Will he be okay?" she yelled.

"He has atom bombs in his back closet, he'll be fine," Mathew yelled. They ducked under a metal barrier before it clanged closed behind them.

Chapter Twenty-Three

Charity ran with Matthew into the falling dark, a stitch in her side throbbed with each step. She slipped on the smooth floor, flailed her arms, caught herself and ran faster. There was no choice.

Matthew grabbed her hand, dragging her along. She stumbled as the ground abruptly became rougher. The slick cement floor broke into smaller and smaller chunks. She tripped on stones and stumbled on gravel.

Charity guessed that they emerged a good three kilometers from the explosion. They struck out across the fields until they came to a long narrow track.

"Now all we need is a ride." Mathew slowed his pace. They trudged together in much the same way as they had trudged earlier in the day.

They jumped out of the way of a truck filled with crates of clucking and cawing chickens.

Mathew let out a shout and the man slowed.

"We need a ride. Where you going?" Mathew thrust a handful of the bills through the half opened window.

The man, who except for the poultry he was transporting, looked like he worked in one of the mines, regarded the two of them, then the bills. "You aren't from here are you?"

"That's why we need to get to San Francisco." Mathew kept his voice even and Charity could tell how much effort he expended to stay calm.

"Got anything to do with that explosion at the old lab?"

"No," Charity stepped up to the truck and flashed her best and what she hoped, winning smile. "We want to see the Great Unification. Do you know anything about the explosion?"

"Don't know, dangerous to fire up anything around here." He nodded to the cargo in the back of this truck. "We make the biggest eggs in the state, so it's not all bad."

Looking satisfied that he delivered the most succinct agricultural lecture he could, he took the bills from Matthew and gestured to the back of the truck.

Matthew jumped on the bed and offered his hand to Charity. "Come on, every traveler needs a chicken bus story."

Charity clutched at the thick wires of the chicken cages and tried to keep from bouncing against the rough walls of the pick up truck as the driver seemed to target every pothole. She longed to stop the bouncing and at least stretch her cramped legs and flex her fingers, but Matthew wouldn't hear of it.

"This is better than we could hope for!" He yelled over the rattle of the truck and the clucking on the chickens. "He won't stop!"

"Where are we headed?"

"Back to San Francisco. That's what you want, right?" He glanced at his phone. "We have twelve hours."

* * * *

Clive managed to hit the intended target and not a uranium container for which Martin was grateful.

However Clive steadfastly refused to move past the frightening barriers to check on their work. "This whole field is radioactive. You remember what happened when we traversed that radioactive lake in *Game of Drones*?"

"Melted down to our boots."

"That was a nice touch, leaving the boots intact," Clive said.

"So, we agree, this is not a good day to melt?"

"Not a good day at all."

"Think they got away?" asked Martin, frowning.

"If they're alive, and I still think that great grenade I threw got them, but let's pretend they're alive, then yes, they got away. How else would we continue the game?"

"Agreed." Martin watched his brother fold up the launcher and packed it away. "We need to return to the City anyway. Have things to do."

* * * *

Well short of midnight, Charity and Matthew disembarked from their clucking, feathery transport.

"We can still get food and a room." Matthew took her hand and pulled her towards the closest towering building.

Charity found he was wrong. It took them two hours before they found a rundown motel. It only had a free room because the previous occupant had suddenly died.

"You're lucky, no rooms in this town, not with the Grand Convergence tomorrow." The hotel clerk shoved two heavy old-fashioned keys to Matthew.

"Food?" Charity asked faintly.

"Farbers in the rooms." The man nodded. "The charge will go on your bill."

Her stomach growled. Still she would have very much liked her last meal here to be of better quality than something pumped out of a replicator.

Matthew preceded her into the room. "It's not fancy, but it will do for a few hours."

Not fancy, Charity shook her head—dreary. The carpet had been worn to the wood floor underneath. The bedspread barely covered the double bed, and it didn't look like it had been cleaned in years. A white replicator, its screen glowing blue, was the newest and most sanitary feature of the room.

"What's your pleasure?" Matthew dropped his bag and walked to the machine.

"Not chicken."

He nodded. "Steak and baked potatoes, from the classic line." He pressed a few buttons and the machine started to hum.

Charity tried not to wolf down the tender beef and creamy potato—almost as good as dirt food—but it was difficult to be a demure young daughter when she was starving.

"This is pretty good," she managed to utter between bites.

"I like a woman who eats." He handed her a wine glass. "Uncle Hugh doesn't think you can really create good wine in a replicator, but it's the best we can do. Hey, slow down. It's like you're eating your last meal."

"With any luck. The replicated food of the future doesn't taste the same."

He nodded. "Do you think you accomplished what you came to do?"

"To be honest I have no idea. It could be talking with Dranit. It could be telling the girls not to stay home." She pointed at him. "It could be you."

"It could be the death of those girls at the club," he said.

She winced at the memory. That was too high a price. No

matter what the outcome. Even with that reality hanging over her, dinner made Charity feel more human. She eyed the bed with distaste. Maybe with Matthew, it wouldn't be so bad...

"So, are you ready?" He rose and offered his hand.

Charity felt the blush rise up and suffuse her cheeks. "Ready?"

"For the rest of our adventure." He moved to his bag. "Here, I got you something."

Charity drained her wine glass and waited, not sure what to do with her hands.

He pulled out a spangled corset, matching skirt and high red platform pumps.

"Really?" Charity shrank from the offending red shoes. What choice did she really have? She knew she needed to reach the Duck and Screw tomorrow, but Mathew could easily delay her. There were the men on their motorcycles to consider...and Dranit for that matter. Or had he given up? Her heart twisted at the thought. But Dranit was the bad guy. And Matthew?

"Why don't you wear them?" It was a feeble joke, at this point, all she had.

"Because it will work better if you do." He tossed the bustier to her and she automatically caught it.

"Work how?" She turned it over in her hands. It was ironic that wearing something so gaudy would actually help her blend in. What a strange past.

Matthew dropped the shoes. "Don't get all coy on me now. I'll take you to the pub, but I need you to do something for me in exchange."

"Exchange?" Her mind raced to their moment together in the bunker. Exchange for sex? The outfit would suggest so.

Her eyes fixed on the shoes while she calculated the physics of staying upright while wearing them. Or did the girls wear the shoes while on the bed? Her mind whirled trying to latch on to a coherent thought.

He regarded her for a minute, all the sensuality and affection wiped from his tone. "I need to get into the Knight office, and I, we, need to do it now while they're distracted by this Unification thing."

"It's not a thing. It's the greatest peace treaty the world has ever known."

"Did you get that right on the test?"

"Of course."

"Help me, and I will take you back to the Duck and Screw."
She remained silent.

"Do you want to find it yourself?"

She glanced up at him, looming over her. No, she wasn't entirely sure about him either. Ah, maybe it was easier to have your parents choose your mate. She wasn't doing such a great job by herself.

She picked up the shoes and dangled them from the skinny straps. "I'll change shoes when we get there."

They were either lucky, or Matthew had been planning this "exchange" for a long time. They emerged into the frantic crowd. The energy had ratcheted up to a fever pitch. More and more people coupled in doorways, corners, even in the middle of the street. Women with bare breasts and bare bottoms screamed and danced on cars. Men leaned from open windows calling to people below to come up for one last night of fun.

She could have been naked and no one would have given her a second glance.

Charity kept her head down and followed Matthew to the wharf where a night ferry, filled with revelers, was just about to launch.

Halfway across the Bay, Charity finally ducked into the toilet to change. She wobbled her way back out to Matthew. Without her leggings her legs were exposed and very cold. She vowed to never wear a short skirt again.

The TV screens in the lounge blared. Newscasters announced this historic occasion. *All to happen at noon today.* But the City was no stranger to the historic. Used often as the central cast member in a variety of films, San Francisco had even hosted the 2080 summer Olympics, the coldest summer Olympics on record.

Charity ignored the looks of the men as she walked to join Matthew. He grinned as she approached. "Nice, you look good in heels."

"Oh, thanks so much. It was one of my goals on this trip, to look good in heels."

He squeezed her waist and kissed her temple. "Think of it as a disguise."

The wind whipped her hair around her cheeks and fog curled around her and chilled her to the bone. She missed the baggy dresses of the future. The future that was about to begin.

Chapter Twenty-Four

After the ferry docked, the now tired and subdued crowd with dropping feathers and dragging noisemakers headed silently to the parking lot. Charity and Matthew followed the group, allowing the dark parking lot to swallow them up. Charity was certain no one took any notice.

Feet aching in the red shoes, Charity walked with Matthew for only a few blocks to an unremarkable business park. A multi-storied building loomed before them, blocking access to the bay beyond. Charity imagined that the back of the building commanded a stunning view of the City sky line. Lights flared from the windows but the streets were dark and devoid of people.

"That's it," Matthew whispered. One lone guard stood before double doors decorated with flamboyant Ks. "You need to get the keys."

"You didn't plan ahead?"

"I'm more of a seat of the pants kind of guy, now go." He pushed her forward.

She wobbled on the unfamiliar red heels trying to keep her balance. She approached the guard and batted her eyes.

"Hi, I lost—" She kept her eyes trained on him and resisted looking up at the cameras she knew were posted all around the building. Cameras were always scattered around the perimeter of any building. "...my keys."

The guard looked her up and down and licked his lips. He didn't seem worried about the cameras watching them.

She tensed but kept her smile in place. "I just need to dash in and get my purse." She opened her arms to demonstrate her loss. "Of course my keys are in the purse." She batted her eyes so vigorously she thought she'd fly away.

"It may cost you. It's pretty late." He stepped towards her and she steeled herself not to automatically shrink back. "Maybe we should go inside together." He leered. As the guard reached for Charity, she cringed back in spite of herself. She tried not to look at Matthew immediately behind the man.

Matthew hit the guard over the head. The man fell with a thud, just missing Charity.

"Good girl." Matthew dragged the guard by the feet and hid him in the surrounding bushes. "Let's go."

"You know the cameras recorded everything." Charity nodded to the black lens she knew so well. Security hadn't changed much in a handful of decades.

Mathew looked up at the camera and waved, then busied himself searching the guard for the key card. "Doesn't matter, most of the Knight security is busy at Union Square, and by the time they see this, by the time they figure out where I am, it will be too late."

"Too late for what?"

Matthew pulled out a key card and slapped it up against the door frame. The door opened and they dashed inside.

"Too late to stop me, or us." The lobby was empty and seemingly unprotected. Charity looked for cover but didn't find much to conceal them in the glass and tile entrance. With a sigh, she slipped off the offending shoes and let them dangle from her fingers as she followed Matthew up the stairs. "How do you know where to go?" She panted, as the rough grid of the stairs bit into her bare feet.

"Been practicing all my life. Kind of like searching for the Holy Grail. Appropriate for today, don't you think?"

But the Holy Grail was never found. Breaking and entering, this was his big goal? He could burgle Knight Industries any time, why tonight?

He paused and pulled her up a section of steps. "Don't fall behind."

It seemed to take forever until Matthew was satisfied. He pushed through the door marked seven and they emerged into another long hall. This one, Charity was pleased to note, was carpeted. A banner saying *Knight Industries: Conveyer of the Convergence* was strung over double doors at the very end of the corridor. They quickly reached the far door, Charity relishing every step on the soft carpet.

Matthew pressed the stolen card against the door frame under the banner. The right hand door swung open without a sound.

He gestured for her to follow. They walked into a large room lined with closed doors.

"Like an office building," she said quietly. Matthew glanced back, surprised.

"Offices are on TV." She shrugged. "Father said his office in the RC looked like the offices we see in the movies." She bit her lip, not wanting to reveal anything more.

"You can be anything in the Reality Cloud," Matthew murmured.

He tried a door at random and it yielded to his touch. Charity followed and glanced into the spacious room.

"I'm not an expert," she said. "I'm not from this time. But why are these doors not secured? Aren't they supposed to be protecting important information?"

"They don't know what will be important." Matthew moved from door to door. "But you might."

He pushed the last door, a big heavy oak door. They entered a sanctuary of luxury and opulence.

"The family headquarters," Matthew said.

He strode confidently to the huge desk centered in the room. Charity lingered and took in the real paintings decorating the walls. The lights brightened and dimmed in synch with their movements. As Charity knew, every light triggered a new camera, recording their every move. Matthew must know this, and Charity couldn't fathom why he was so unconcerned.

"They'll see us, won't they?" She waved and smiled at the corner of the room, out of old habit and new defiance.

In the same spirit, Matthew raised his middle finger and swept his other hand over the desk top. A screen appeared. He swiped at the transparent surface, rejecting and placing various files and images to one side.

His face was intense as he searched.

"Damn." He opened and closed files and images at a rapid rate. "Come here, take a look at these."

Charity obeyed, still not sure of her role. It looked to her like he was just scrambling around icons and files. "There," she pointed to three linked files. "I recognize the RC logo."

He smiled and pulled out a flat card the size of the key card. He inserted the card below the desktop and dropped the three files into the card icon. Matthew pulled out the card and considered it, then tucked the slim plastic into his shoe.

* * * *

"God damn, son of a bitch."

Stephen Knight heard the alarm and rolled out of bed.

"What honey?" His wife stirred but did not join him into the chilly room. "Your favorite grandchild is not doing his job," Stephen snarled. "There's been a breach. Damn it, this must be it. Right during the Great Unification, son of a bitch has impeccable timing."

"What do we care? It won't affect us, come back to bed."

He glanced back at her in contempt. "You never did get it did you? It's not just about controlling the present. If anyone can succeed today, then everyone can succeed tomorrow. Can you imagine the chaos of the future if everyone can change the past? If everyone did return to change the past? If they thought it was easy?" He smacked the side of his temple so hard he hurt himself. He barked the Kahn brothers' name.

"I can't think about those things so early in the morning," she complained.

He regarded her inert form. There were days when he second guessed all his choices. And his beautiful wife was at the top of that perpetual list.

* * * *

Charity clattered down the stairs behind Matthew all while questions formed and spiraled in her head. Why wasn't this place more secure? Was this a trap or was Matthew meant to distract Stephen Knight at a critical point in history? Was she?

She raced to keep pace with Matthew, her shoes clanking against the metal railing.

She focused on the back of Matthew's head, well-proportioned, beautiful. Yet another idea was dawning on her. No, she was crazy, and obviously not as good at history as she thought. Who knew real life would be an essay test?

Alarms bells, louder and more insistent than even the alarms at Hugh's bunker shocked the emerging thought from her head.

The first guard was still unconscious, but they reasonably anticipated more alert men were on the way.

They slowed and walked carefully from the building as if just taking a stroll. Charity caught a shadow move in the park that surrounded the building. She quickly slipped on her shoes and staggered next to Matthew as if she was drunk.

Two guards rounded the corner and almost leveled their guns until Charity lurched and almost pushed Matthew to the sidewalk.

"Oops. Oh honey, I'm sorry. You're supposed to catch me," she playfully slapped his check.

Matthew tightened his grip around her waist and kissed her hard on the mouth. The guards approached, weapons lowered. One smirked and made a lewd comment about their immediate future, that, thankfully, Charity didn't fully understand. They slowly passed the guards. Matthew kissed her check, checking over her shoulder as he did.

"Keep staggering, they're watching your ass."

"My what?"

"Just keep moving, that corset brings out just about the best of everything you have to offer."

"That's good?" She carefully tilted against him. Appearing intoxicated was more difficult than she thought.

"Are you kidding? I can't even control myself and I have sobering evidence digging into my instep as we speak."

Matthew took them back to the ferry dock. A line of auto-cars glinted under one street lamp. Matthew waved his phone over the driver's window and opened one.

"They'll track that," she pointed out.

"It only crosses the bridge. And unless you want to walk, we don't have much of a choice."

She was not interested in walking across the impossibly high bridge in these equally impossible heels.

Matthew climbed in the driver's seat and Charity slid into the passenger's side. The car would not be hurried, but sedately drove from the ferry to the bridge. In the spirit of every experience being her very last, Charity rolled down her window and leaned out. The fog had already rolled in, covering just the bridge. Cold damp hair chilled her cheeks and made her close her eyes against the onslaught. So much damp air! The orange bridge arches, streaked with dark rust loomed over her in the yellow-tinged night.

It was fantastic. She, Charity Northquest, was on the bridge the very last night of its existence. Who in her time could say that? She wanted to let out a whoop, but knew it would be too much. After a few minutes, she reluctantly drew in when she could not longer feel her nose.

"Get that out of your system?" Matthew stared straight

ahead. "Are you sure you want to return?"

The orange arches flashed overhead, the lights were dim, the city glowed across the water as if it was on fire, or in the throes of an all-night party.

She boldly reached out and stroked his cheek. "I wish there was some way to make this forever, to make our lives together last." She knew she'd have to memorize him since nothing was going home with her. Nothing but her memories that, with any luck, will be completely irrelevant. Still, they belonged to her. She hoped she could keep them when she returned.

Chapter Twenty-Five

Charity knew most of the morning would be spent in ceremony. Dignitaries of every country and heads of all the churches, temples, mosques, synagogues, forests, everyone, would assemble at the Saint Francis hotel. The security was unparalleled. The government, represented by the President and Vice President assured the safety of all dignitaries and visitors alike.

Video cameras, phones, and any other devices, were forbidden. This was a day of history for living memory only. Just like it used to be. As if they were all here to witness the Second Coming and only their eyes and their memories would do.

Matthew opened his phone and handed it to Charity. "You're worried about the Unification, in just a few hours the treaties will be signed, and we will become one big happy monochromatic family."

Charity watched on the phone's screen all the men already positioned around the square. It was safe, but the building would not sustain the coming quake—she squinted at the video of the square itself. It looked clear, just like in her history video. Yet if there were no cameras allowed how did those videos come to be made?

She leaned back in her passenger seat and hoped this idea of soft cushions in vehicles would survive into the next century. *Cushions and springs, so much better than hard plastic.*

The car circled a number of blocks before its automatic system would allow them to disembark. Matthew wanted to override the system and double-park, but it was too crowded to even do that.

In first year history, all girls learned that the Great Convergence happened on Union Square, named for the great Unification. There, Stephen Knight and Makepeace Wilson brokered the most sweeping confluence of religions known to man.

Charity and Matthew pushed through the throng, passing

monitor after monitor all flashing updates on the Convergence. An old photograph of the hotel entrance alternated with photos of Stephen Knight, Makepeace, the Pope, preachers, rabbis, they were all here. The announcer shifted and fidgeted with his token piece of paper before him on the news desk.

"This just in. According to our source, the venue for the Convergence has been changed. Crowds are shifting to the Embarcadero, all along Crissy Field. If you are in the area, stay there, traffic is at a standstill down Van Ness. Jane?"

A young woman, working hard to keep her balance against the shifting crowd, nodded then spoke, "According to sources who we can't mention here, the Vice President has just announced the hotel is too small to accommodate the growing crowd. Knight Industries has volunteered to transport the delegates to the more open field. The spokesperson for the President has no comment at this time."

The screen flashed to a long beach now packed with bodies. Everyone waved to the helicopters hovering overhead, cameras trained on the edge of the bay.

"No," Charity watched the TV screen in growing horror.

"It's just a last minute move," Matthew glanced at the screen.

"But it was in the square, the square outside saved them."

"Saved them from what?"

Charity glanced at the time at the base of the TV screen. There was no time for all those people to hustle back to the center of the city.

"Come on. Let's get you home." He pulled on her arm, but she resisted.

She stared at the screen completely transfixed. *They didn't know.* Her mind raced trying to justify all the historical stories she had learned against what she was seeing with her own eyes. The Knight family did move the Great Unification ceremonies and meetings from inside the old hotel to the relative safety of the square. It was a critical move. It was a history-making move. It was not happening as it should.

"What did the Knight Family do to earn the right of perpetual governance?" She ticked the answers off on her fingers. "Organized the Reality Cloud, employed all the men, saved the Great Unification from disaster." The wrong choice had been Foster democracy. Why did she always remember the wrong answer?

She couldn't turn away from the screen: 11:45 a.m. More and more people surged to the water's edge.

"No one is protesting," she said.

He reached out his hand to help move her along, but the sidewalk moved instead. The ground buckled and rolled under them. Charity shrank back against the building and looked fearfully at the overhang. The sidewalk shifted, lifted, under her feet. How could solid ground suddenly become like liquid? She pressed against the rough building and shut her eyes, preferring not to see her own end.

Matthew kept his balance, and managed to not be thrown to the ground. The TV screen banged against the glass store window with a horrible noise, but the glass held.

"Look at that." He pulled Charity up so she could see the video of the Golden Gate Bridge swaying, and then righting itself. The camera panned back to the beach over the exclamations and protests of the newscaster.

"A 6.5!" the newscaster bellowed, all pretense of calm authority gone.

"6.7," Charity said.

"You knew this was coming?"

Around them doors slammed. People who weren't already out reveling one last time, emerged from their homes and looked up at the sky. They turned to their neighbors, gesturing and talking.

"They were all outside, gathered just far enough from the falling debris. Safe," Charity repeated the *New Bible Verse*.

The newscast panned back to Crissy field. Obviously, there were no buildings along the beach so there was nothing that could injure the delegates, everyone was safe. Knight, who looked much older than the photographs on TV, shouted through the PA system. "Don't panic, see? We're right, this is the most righteous thing we can do—our One True God demands it!"

The crowd roared.

"I guess nothing can stop it." Charity fought down her growing panic; it wasn't over.

* * * *

Martin and his brother inched slowly around the edge of the crowd, intent on their quarry. Their boss had called it

Plan B. They didn't understand the idea of Plan B but they did know this hit would be the stuff of legends. After much soul-searching, even Martin was ready for immortality.

"They could have picked up the beach, this being such a momentous occasion," Clive observed.

"What?"

"The beach, they could have cleaned it up. Look at all that junk, rusting and rotting—it's a disgrace."

"They didn't know—" Martin stopped and really looked at the beach his brother indicated. A long, a very long, swath of muddy beach disappeared into the far surf, populated by what could only be decades of debris all mashed together in unrecognizable lumps. Rusted parts of ships and recent beer cans glinted in the sun.

"There isn't a beach—" he began.

A far roar stopped him.

"We're in big trouble." He grabbed his brother and turned away from the rising water, but the water was fast and the crowd acted like another implacable wall. Unbelievably, people were moving towards the edge of the water. Like his brother, they were fascinated with the newly-expanded beach.

"We have to get out." He pulled desperately at Clive.

"But our mission—" His brother stayed solidly in place; he was always the larger of the two.

Martin pulled again, but it was too late. A wall of water that had paused at the Golden Gate only long enough to build more force, broke and heaved towards them like a flat indomitable mountain. Martin couldn't see through it, or around it. All he could see was the fearsomely advancing fifteen-foot high water. He opened his mouth to utter some ridiculous instructions like duck or hold on but before he could utter a sound—the wave slammed into the crowd.

* * * *

Charity moaned.

The color drained from Matthew's face as he watched the carnage on the TV. "We need to move."

"Oh, One True God. He didn't save them."

"Come on, let's just get you back, maybe you can tell the truth."

"Oh really? Have you tried that lately?" she shot back.

He just shook his head and led her from the horrific images flashing on the screen.

The Duck and Screw was only a block away. She could have found it herself, but she was too shocked to chastise Matthew. What had happened?

They approached the bar slowly, Charity almost reluctantly. But there were no motorcycle men lurking around, no cops, no officers. The buildings in this section of town didn't look too damaged from the quake. Charity placed her hand on the cool wood—it had survived of course, the whole neighborhood survived. .

Mathew pulled out his phone and glanced at the time. "Won't be happy hour for a while. Maybe never."

"A trap?" Charity looked around at the empty streets.

Mathew shook his head. "I don't think so."

He pushed open the heavy door decorated with a stained-glass insert and ushered Charity through.

The place was empty except for one man at the bar hunched over a martini glass.

"Dranit," Charity said quietly. He looked up as they entered.

Mathew pushed Charity behind him, but Dranit makes no move towards them. He gestured with a nod of his head to the TV screen over the bar. "You heard?"

Charity glanced up. All she saw was mayhem, people screaming and running, jagged pieces of pier, collapsed buildings, bodies. A helicopter had risen above the fray and an intrepid photographer captured on film the remains of the Golden Gate Bridge. A voice-over explained that the wave had rushed the bay, narrowed and built up at the Golden Gate and pushed into the bay with immeasurable force.

"An historic moment." Dranit finished his drink and raised his hand. "Two more, for my friends.

"If I remember correctly, the President was killed today," Dranit mused. "I never knew how."

The bartender slid two martinis, one to Charity, one to Matthew. Matthew knocked his back in one swallow. Charity sipped hers. It wasn't sweet, but it wasn't bad. Perhaps a person needed time to develop a taste for real alcohol. The bartender slid another drink to Dranit.

Matthew set down his glass and regarded his adversary. "How do you know?"

Dranit shrugged and gestured to the screen. "My grandfather thought he knew enough to manipulate events." He took a sip.

Matthew narrowed his eyes. "So what?"

"So what..." Dranit fished the large olive from his drink and bit it in half. "...is that the cheat codes you took such trouble to get, don't work. None of the codes work."

"What codes?" Charity stepped around Matthew and stood between them.

"Tell her." Dranit finished the olive and regarded them both calmly. "Tell her what you were really doing."

Charity turned to Matthew. He ducked his head and didn't meet her eyes. "We were told to look for you, that you would help our family get ahead. Since everything in the Cloud would be a game, I figured whomever had the cheat codes, would win."

Dranit laughed. "That's the beauty of it. There is *no* win."

"It's not a game?" Matthew gestured for another drink.

"Oh, it's a game all right, a violent, sexual, political game. War on an unprecedented, unending scale because no one gets killed." He glanced at Charity. "It's quite addicting, just ask any man in your time—but there is no win."

Matthew slumped. Charity placed a hand on his shoulder. Why wouldn't he want the advantage for his family?

"I considered burning the building," Dranit said conversationally, nodding to the bartender. "But I realized that wouldn't really make a difference."

"For time travel?" Matthew asked.

Dranit nodded and drained his martini. "There were stories about energy and time convergences in the western states, some people even worship there. The energy and channeling won't be altered for lack of a building, at least according to my mother."

"Your mother?"

"You remember the riots? During the Great Celebration?" Dranit locked his gaze on her.

She nodded.

"They broke into our house. At the last minute, my mother tossed me back," he gestured with his head, "here. To save me."

She blinked back a surge of tears. A child, hurled into the void.

"You told your grandfather everything," Matthew said.

Dranit glanced at the TV screen. "I was only eight." He looked directly at Charity. "Turns out I didn't tell him everything."

Doubt overwhelmed her. Matthew had insisted she dress oddly and help with breaking and entering for his own purpose. Dranit had only fed and housed her, helped her. Charity slowly eased away from Matthew murmuring something about the toilet.

Matthew gave her a serious look. She let her hand linger on his balled up fist. The tears now coursed down her cheeks. She slowly, as casually as she could, worked her way past Dranit.

Dranit reached out and grabbed her arm. She locked eyes with him. "Before you go, did our friend here tell you?"

She stiffened and glanced at Mathew, who did not move.

"We all have our family secrets. His began in nineteenth century Nevada."

She searched Matthew's face. He studied the worn wooden bar and would not look up.

"Tell me her name, your ancestor," she commanded.

"Mirabella," Matthew whispered.

Her shoulders slumped. Dranit slowly uncurled his fingers. Stiffly she made her way down the hall to the utility closet. Neither man protested, what would be the point of stopping her? She had failed, as epically as the tsunami had triumphed.

She shut the closet door, feeling in the dark, working towards the coldest spot in the tiny space. She remembered the four steps to the door when she first scrambled up steeling herself for an adventure. Her heart had not been as heavy back then. But a long time ago, far in the future, she hadn't known she had a heart.

* * * *

Her ears rang, a singing coursed through her bones as if every molecule in her body vibrated at a range she could not hear, only feel.

She closed her eyes, or thought she did. The dark engulfed her and rattled her like dried beans in a can.

She couldn't breathe. She struggled to keep her arms close to her sides, her legs clamped together, hoping that she would be one big mass and not a collection of dangling parts ready to be picked off by the force of the trip.

After what seemed like a century in the cold and dark, a faint light glowed around the edges of her gripped closed eyes.

She finally stopped vibrating and fell in a heap on the floor. A least this one was a bit cleaner.

Chapter Twenty-Six

She tentatively flexed her fingers, attached. She wiggled her toes. She was pretty sure they were attached.

The money belt was still in place. The corset was tight and still very uncomfortable. She absently rubbed the inside of her arm and cautiously opened the door. No sounds of gunfire or bombs. She looked both ways. The narrow hall was deserted. She listened, but did not hear the crowd outside. Was she in yet another time? It was so quiet. The door at the end of the hall—*Exit*—was solid, giving her no helpful information.

She squared her shoulders. There was no point in hiding, or hesitating. She heard the low murmur of a television, unmistakable in any time.

She paused at the toilet. No, she was fine and frankly didn't even care what she looked like. She didn't move. Okay, she did care.

She ducked into the toilet and flipped on the light. Well yes, she did look worse for the experience. Her hair was blown and tangled, and black. That's right, she had dyed it. *Fat lot of good that did.* She smoothed the short strands as best she could. There wasn't much she could do about the dark circles under her eyes or the scratch on her arm. She adjusted the bright red busier and glanced with dismay at her bare feet. Oh boy, she looked like a prostitute after her last client.

How did she know what a prostitute looked like?

Charity dashed water on her face and slapped some color into her cheeks.

"You look like you've been through a couple natural disasters," she told her reflection. "Time to discover the rest of it, if there's more." She wasn't sure she could handle more.

She cautiously stepped into the bar. The floor was sticky against her bare feet. Well, that wasn't unexpected.

A sign over the long wooden bar proclaimed *The Oldest Pub in the City*. She scanned for cameras, but did not see any tiny blinking eyes. Perhaps by now, the surveillance equipment was hidden in the very paint of the building. She tried to recall if she knew that.

Never mind. The place was familiar, because of course, she had left it only a minute ago. But instead of suspicious glances, or disgruntled rumblings, the handful of patrons scattered around the bar, paid no attention to her.

No Dranit. No Matthew. She touched the spot where Dranit had sat, only minutes before.

A young man behind the bar wiped glasses and stacked them on the illuminated shelf above. Charity slipped onto a high stool and rested her arms on the bar.

"What will you have?"

"Everything," she answered. She scanned the bottles but then asked for what she, essentially, had already been drinking. "Martini."

He nodded and pulled a bottle of vodka down.

"Looking for someone?" He slid the martini to her and she took it without hesitation.

"Because..." His blue eyes twinkled. "Nice girls don't ordinarily come into the bar at this hour, even fewer order an old drink like a martini."

She smiled back. "What makes you think I'm a nice girl?"

She sipped her drink. It tasted familiar, almost comforting. She now understood why humans still made drinks, still drank. Matthew's face rose before her. She blinked back sudden tears. So this was the sacrifice. She hoped Dranit had survived his grandfather's wrath. She silently toasted all that went before, the Grandmothers, the Mothers who knew but chose not to go back. She toasted the women who tried, decade after decade, to change things through the past because the present wasn't pay attention.

The bartender turned on the faucet and washed two more glasses. She toasted to the running water.

A man at one of the tables slipped off his seat and approached her. "In all the gin joints in all the world." The young man hopped onto the stool next to her. "She walks into mine."

"I'm sorry, do I know you?" Charity pulled back a bit.

The bartender laughed. "Don't mind him; he studies old films."

"Have I been very bad?" Her tone was hopeful.

The man behind the bar snorted and the handsome man laughed.

"Charity, right?" He tipped his head. "Your hair is different."

She put her hand up and felt her hair.

"Understand, we just had that one image. You had more purple in your hair. Terrible fashion, but it was the thing to do at the time."

Her eyes widened in shock. He nodded. "That's right. That picture taken in the club. The kids still do that, you know? They like the full body contact, the risk of personal infection. Face-to-face." He shook his head. "That hasn't changed."

She nodded slowly, still not quite understanding.

"Sorry. Lucky me. I can return to college, now that you've been found."

"Found?"

He pulled out a battered envelope from his pocket and handed it to her. "I could spend all day and explain, but you probably can connect the dots pretty easily yourself."

"Oh." He tapped her gently on the arm. "Welcome back to the Twenty-Second Century."

He moved away, softly whistling. She glanced down at the envelope, but didn't open it.

The bartender slid another martini to her and she tried to resist downing it in one gulp.

Behind her was the very table where Dranit sat, waiting for her to emerge. The lights and the beams were unchanged. Could she retreat back into the utility closet? What would happen if she did?

The pull was irresistible. Could she return? The world seemed perfectly fine at the very least, dry. She could go back and find Matthew. What had happened after she left, and why hadn't either man stopped her? She shivered and took another sip. Perhaps in this life she was an alcoholic. She didn't even care.

A group behind her laughed and clicked beer glasses.

But returning to the past wasn't much of an option, really. She carefully slit open the fragile envelope.

She pulled out two certificates—the paper was so creased that three dusty lines intersected the writing. But it was clear what they were: A certificate for 1,000 shares of Knight Industries, and another for 1,000 shares of Singh Productions.

They didn't know who would win either.

"I have something else." The bartender pulled a small book

from his pocket. "A long time ago a guy named Knight left this here, the message said it would be about a hundred years before you returned." He looked up at the clock. "About right."

"You don't seem very surprised." She took the small package.

"I own a bar in San Francisco called the Duck and Screw, how surprised do you think I get?" He arched an eyebrow and returned to organizing the glasses. She carefully unwrapped a small notebook with a faded *B of A* on the cover. Another note tucked in.

You may need a little income and a room of your own.—Dranit.

The book was filled with account names and passwords.

She took the package and slipped it under her bustier.

Wiping her tears, she surveyed the dingy bar. What had she expected to find? Matthew himself? To fall in love with the great-grandson of her best friend?

That only happened in books.

"Excuse me, I have one more question." She leaned on the bar and addressed the young man. "Is there a shoe store near here?"

Chapter Twenty-Seven

Even with new shoes and a general idea of where the train station was located, Charity's dislocation was overwhelming. What had changed? Had she changed?

She glanced at the people as she hiked back to the train station. They looked much like the people she had just left, happier maybe? The women at least were out on their own—no hats, no long, covering dresses. But she was still in the City.

She headed for the train station, led partially by instinct and partially because the route was well-marked by signs. She couldn't resist taking a moment and lifting her face to the setting sun. It was warm, still unusual judging by the other walkers who stopped and like her, lifted their faces to the light.

Was she dreaming? Or had she dreamed all that went before, all the adventure, the time travel?

It had been a pretty long dream. Still, she never hurt in a dream, or gone hungry in a dream, or turned down a boy in a dream, not even her imagination would have done that.

The train was new and fast—fifteen minutes to Sonoma University, twenty to Santa Rosa, that was her home now?

The train ran on reverse rails, slung under the Golden Gate Bridge like a carnival ride, but she couldn't remember if she read about carnival rides or if she'd been on one.

"I'm so glad it was rebuilt. It's such a symbol. It was the first thing the president commissioned after the wave," a passenger said.

Charity nodded.

The train zipped through Marin and into Sonoma County. Green hills and lush farms flowed away from the train. *Dirt farms.* Did they not use replicated food? She was tempted to walk though the train to see if there were Fabers at the end of the train car, but she didn't want to call attention to herself any more than necessary.

She fingered the old leather book. What would her parents say? And was there any way she could tell them? She glanced up at the roof of the train but couldn't detect any cameras, which meant nothing.

The train raced through green and brown hills and low white buildings. In the seat behind Charity, a small girl struggled over her tablet, spelling out names first, then working on a quiz. Her mother, dressed in tight-fitting leggings and a loose tunic, leaned over her child.

"Remember you learned about the earthquake and flood?" The mother asked.

"Which one?" the little girl whined.

The train sped through more fields and low trees. It looked much like the projections on the city walls, but this time, this time they were real, she could see the difference, or was she just hopeful? The train climbed and turned a corner, and slowed—the first stop.

Charity checked the screen above the exit doors:

Sonoma University. Tonight, Doctor Betsy Nite at the Knute Library—Is Time Travel Possible?

Out the window the former village buildings looked the same, but instead of empty space and a few tenacious trees and bushes, the place was neatly tended, even attractive, and populated by city dwellers, all looking much the same as the people she passed in San Francisco.

Something tugged at her memory. Was she a student here? Charity wanted to attend the lecture, she knew that. Did she know Doctor Nite? She wanted to, but there had been a family conflict and she had been disappointed.

Oh, too bad. I hope that was my only problem.

A smile spread over Charity's face. She had changed it. Even if it was this one thing, she had changed something.

She bounced on the cushioned seat and tried not to allow her euphoria to get the best of her. She also knew, vaguely, that as far as her family was concerned, she was in a lot of trouble. With any luck, they'd ground her. She could use the rest.

The second stop was at the center train station, which Charity gratefully recognized. It had not changed all that much, still big and a bit dusty, but the trains whooshing in and out made no sound.

Charity exited and paused, allowing the other passengers to move forward. The little girl skipped next to her mother clutching her tablet. The last time Charity had entered here was from underground. She glanced at the barred tunnel as she passed. It didn't look used, not in many years.

An enormous analog clock hung in the lobby of the station. Seven p.m. She had been gone since two p.m. Assuming this was the same day. The time and date crawl under the clock said same day. She shook her head, it wasn't possible. But of course, Mirabella had said it was very possible.

Charity wound her way through their city. The warehouses were gone, replaced by more graceful buildings that, as far as she could tell, were real, not projections. Cars zoomed by her, some autocars and some piloted by actual people. Men and women walked to their homes. The sky was blue, bluer than it had a right to be. She blinked. Was it blue or just a blue projection? She couldn't tell. She peered down streets to determine if the wall around the town still stood, but she couldn't figure that out either.

Her house did not shimmer. It looked remarkably solid. Of course, she didn't know if this was still her house. She hesitated and then figured, *what the hell*, and grasped the door handle.

"There you are!" Her mother opened the door so quickly the handle jerked from Charity's hand. She glared at Charity, who in turn stood stock still in shock. Never mind that her mother's hair was uncovered...it was dyed a brilliant purple-red color and fell around her face in waves. Her eyes sparkled like a young girl's, and the brackets around her mouth were erased. She was beautiful.

"You left your phone at home. I called and called and finally realized that I was calling your bedroom." Her mother didn't stop talking as she opened the door and ushered in the wayward daughter.

"Mother." Charity bowed.

"Oh, as if that will help. You know I have longer days at work since my promotion. You can at least stay around and help your sisters prepare. Faith is beside herself. All those myths of impossible brides are apparently true. Now get up there and tell her that 300 guests are quite enough and inviting her entire class is not possible as the wedding is tomorrow." She pushed back her curls and glared at her daughter.

"No more wandering off. Have a little adult courtesy with your new freedom."

Charity stood stock still under the onslaught, not sure if she was completely appalled or giddily delighted.

Her mother finally focused on Charity. "What the hell are you wearing, and what happened to your hair?"

Charity glanced at the shoes and the tiny skirt. "Costume party. Where's Father?"

"At Knight Industries. Where else would he be?" she snapped.

Charity felt her heart stop. Had they known? Had Dranit told them that about Charity and now they were taking their revenge out on her father? She stopped walking. It was over. Yet...

"Labor talks, the family passion." Her mother rolled her eyes. "I knew his job was important, but a trip to Sacramento Shores right before the wedding? The Gods! Your father and his noblesse oblige. One hundred years of labor support—save the miners—building homes after the tsunami—I know, I know!" She threw up her hands. "This family!" Her straight skirt and short jacket emphasized a figure that was still youthful and vibrant.

Charity composed her face and did her best to looked chagrinned. It was the most words her mother had directed at her since she was a baby.

"Of course. I'm so sorry. Umm, how was your work today?"

"Oh for the Goddess, girl, my work is fine, great! Nancy is a fabulous assistant, helps me so much. Good thing, apparently Faith has been replicating dresses all afternoon and Hope is well, hopeless. At least make your sister choose something, we can't afford all that wasted electricity and materials!"

Charity cautiously made her way up a graceful curving staircase. She followed the sounds of her sisters' voices. Faith's was the loudest and most belligerent. That hadn't changed.

"This one doesn't work well either," Faith said.

"Oh just pick something! You look fabulous." Hope's tone was such that she didn't think her sister looked fabulous at all.

Charity entered the room. Hope was fussing over a resplendent Faith, decked out in a dress so fluffy it seemed to fill the room.

"Really?" Charity paused and regarded her sister. Faith's cheeks were flushed, her eyes glowed, she was the very picture of the happy—perfect—and, Charity noticed immediately, slender bride.

"You are just jealous because no one has proposed." Faith swished the skirts and twisted to see her reflection from all sides. "Does this make my butt look big?"

"It would make an ocean liner look big." Hope ran her hands through her hair and looked at her older sister accusingly.

"And where have you been? Just because you can move around as you please doesn't mean you had to abandon me with bridezilla here."

"I just want to look perfect." Faith pouted.

"You're marrying a Singh. It doesn't get more perfect than that."

"TV coverage," Faith said the words as if that summed up everything. It did. Charity remembered that Faith was marrying into a family that was one of the giants in communications. The Singhs had once been part of an attempt to control all the information, even trading books for electronics, but a fire had prevented them from following through. Books prevailed, and the Singhs shared their empire with the Amazons of the world. But that did not preclude live-casting the whole wedding event to the Singh Subscribers. No wonder Faith was freaked out.

"You don't want to look like Catherine the Second, do you? She's getting so fat!" Her sister sneered.

Charity walked to the bride in question. "I am not jealous and I'm glad you are marrying and you look ridiculous." She regarded the screens on the replicator, much more sophisticated than the past, the number indicating the cost and electricity used had climbed into five digits. No wonder Mother was frantic.

"Let's try this one." Charity pushed a few buttons then nodded to her sister. "Recycle that one."

She hit the button and a sleek dress with a bodice similar to what Charity still wore materialized.

"Oh." Faith handed the rejected ocean liner-like dress to Hope and pulled on the new dress. The bodice, covered with pearls and crystal beads, shimmered in the light. It fit Faith's slender frame perfectly. The satin skirt fell straight and brushed the floor, with just enough length to accommodate high heels.

"Now, that's more like it." Hope eyed her sister. "Just tell me that isn't your idea of a bridesmaid's dress. What did you do to your hair?"

Charity left both sisters to argue about the bridesmaid dresses and escaped to her room, hoping to find some clues about her present condition. Her room was filled with shelves of old-fashion books. She pulled down a copy and was relieved to find it was filled, not a blank prop. Had Hugh died in that explosion? If so, had his project, a project that was not to save books, but rather to control them, also stopped?

Charity contemplated the volume. She owned a thousand shares of Singh Communications, could she sell them if she was related by marriage?

She plopped on her bed. Had she done it? She hadn't started the fire in Hugh's warehouse, but those two men had. But the only reason they had was to get to her. She dropped the book. She couldn't think. She needed, longed for, sleep. A slim screen hovered over a cleared desk. She pressed a button and a purple keyboard appeared on the surface. A screen lit up with options and icons. One was prominent because she had turned off the easy exchange button, as well as, the volume.

Well, that sounded like her.

She pulled open the wardrobe doors and viewed what she had acquired. Favorite things she didn't mind wearing and over. Jackets lined with fake fur that felt soft and luxurious. Shiny sweaters, leggings, long swingy skirts, boots and sandals—both high heeled and flats. Colorful silk scarves. Long coats in brilliant peacock blue and green, all complimentary, all collected to highlight her blue eyes and blond hair. Except she had black hair. She peered in a small mirror. She didn't know if she wanted to change her color back or not.

She gratefully exchanged her hooker ensemble to something more comfortable and ran downstairs to dinner in her bare feet.

Her father returned just in time for their eight p.m. dinner. He was filled with stories about the Central Lake and the Capitol.

"A nephew just arrived to help with labor negotiations, smart fellow. I invited him to the wedding."

Mother stared at her husband. "You've lost your mind, you know that."

"Then I can invite Doctor Nite's brother, which would just make just two extra," Faith put in.

"No one else from school," Hope reminded her sister.

"One more, and it's good for business. Both the Knights and the Singh's have history. But this young man is new and doesn't seem to hold the same long grudges. It'll be fine, you'll see, not everyone who RSVPs comes anyway."

"I suppose you invited your assistant?" Mother looked bent, but not broken. She was quickly typing into her tablet as she spoke. "I'll tell Nancy four, just in case you find someone on the way to the wedding tomorrow."

He grinned at his wife. "Come on, three hundred isn't much at all, and we can afford it."

Mother rolled her eyes, then focused on Charity. "And you, what have you been up to all day?"

Charity reluctantly set down her fork. Dirt food never tasted this good. Not even a hundred years ago, so she was reluctant to stop eating.

"I was working on a school project?" She floated the idea to see if held. It did. Both parents nodded as if that was a reasonable way for her to spend her time. Clearly they weren't going to accept the short answer.

"I was researching the back-to-the-land movement a hundred years ago. It was promoted by the government and Knight Industries to isolate villages and populations and make it easier to manipulate people through water shortages and brown outs." Charity checked the corners of the ceiling— no black camera lens blinked back at her.

"You've been studying history?" her mother wondered at her. "You hate history. Well, good for you. Did you discover that in this country at least, the irony of that approach was that it's very difficult to control a group of broadly scattered people?"

Charity remembered the tunnels, the stolen electricity. She very much knew it was difficult to control people who lived outside the boundaries. She smiled.

"Of course I did."

"Then you know it didn't work." Her father finished his dinner and turned to his middle child. "Just like controlling the mines didn't work, thanks to your great-grandfather."

"Back to your family again!" Her mother drained her glass and poured herself more.

Her father raised his glass, filled with wine. "Here's to the anniversary of the Final Chasm."

Charity raised her glass. "We celebrate this?" Her eyes traveled back to her arm.

Minutes before dinner, Hope inadvertently gave her a clue. "Just because you had your chip removed is no reason to just disappear. I could have used help this afternoon."

"Sorry." *Chip?* She touched her skin again. It would be difficult, returning to a life she only half-remembered. But it was worth it. So worth it.

Hope tucked her hair behind her ear and rolled her eyes. "It must be so interesting to be you."

"Nature spoke, independence and free choice conquered," her father said.

"And the Great Unification didn't happen." Charity tried to make it sound like a statement.

"Of course not. The Knights did a great deal to clean up after the disaster, but no, in the wake of the tsunami, the Unification was impossible to pull off."

Nature. Natural disaster. Charity sighed and sipped her wine.

Chapter Twenty-Eight

For the first time in what seemed like a lifetime, Charity slept for eight hours straight. She didn't wake until Hope bustled in carrying a red dress.

"Up, lazy. We're supposed to arrive early to help greet the guests. Here's your dress; thank the gods it doesn't look like Faith's. She's thrilled by the way. You are the last-minute heroine again." She made a face and ducked back into the hall yelling that they were on their way.

The family piled into a long autodrive car and were whisked away to the wedding site. Charity recognized the park but couldn't say why. Perched dead center of what felt like a very real lawn stood an enormous white tent.

"Like a carnival," she whispered.

An arch over the entrance read Brian and Faith.

"Come on, we have to help." Hope tugged at Charity while Faith was bustled away by the rest of her bridesmaids. Charity didn't recognize any of other girls, but hoped the names and faces would come back to her by the time they all marched down the aisle.

"So old-fashioned." Mother watched as Faith was borne away on a cloud of tulle and silk. "Still it's all the rage right now." She turned to Charity. "Thank the gods you decided on an education."

Charity merely nodded.

She examined the arch. Brian. What would he be? Matthew's great-grandson? Was Matthew alive? Was Dranit alive? No, it was too long ago. She let out a breath that she been holding since she woke. At worst, Brian Singh would resemble his great-grandfather. And inherit their still incomparable wealth. She had rescued Faith from marrying a rapist guard. Good. And Hope was better and sassy. Good. And her parents were well-off. Good. Apparently she was in college. Not even Mirabella herself could have wished for a better ending.

Nancy, dressed in an elegant iridescent suit, walked by holding her fingers to her temple and talking.

"Nancy." Charity made a grab for the woman's arm.

Nancy signed off and turned to Charity. "Oh hello, I'm your mother's new assistant." Nancy held out her hand and Charity shook it.

"I understand you're just finishing your studies at the University," she said kindly.

"I just returned home," Charity said faintly.

"For the wedding, of course." Nancy smiled, then looked at Charity a little oddly. "Have we met?"

Charity pressed her lips together and considered her answer. "No," she said.

After only minutes, Faith was ready to walk. Charity lined up with Hope and the rest of the pretty bridesmaids and clutched the traditional bridesmaid bouquet. Five cameras began recording the procession, livecasting to millions. Charity kept her smile firmly in place but just as she feared, the groom was the spitting image of his grandfather. Brian Singh had the same piercing blue eyes and his hair, despite obvious attempts to tame it, sprang up in curls. Just like his grandfather. A man, she was told, who was long dead. She was afraid to ask if it was due to natural causes.

"Faith looks beautiful doesn't she?" Hope whispered. Charity nodded.

She had thought she was willing to sacrifice everything for her sisters, that was part of the plan right? Her expression softened as the couple pledged to love each other all the days of their lives. How many lives did they have? How many did she?

The reception swirled around her. Buffet tables overflowed with fresh vegetable dishes and thinly sliced meats and cheese. Real, all grown from the ground. They didn't even call it dirt food.

Charity ordered a martini from the bar and watched her sisters dance Her parents circulated and laughed. She didn't remember seeing them laugh together, ever. And now here they were, happy, prosperous. She wondered if that brief conversation with the protesters had made a difference. She smiled at the thought, as if a man, any man, would admit that some young girl had inspired a life-altering course of action.

Charity watched Hope sashay across the dance floor, but

then her eyes were inextricably drawn to another figure. She sucked in her breath in shock. Before she could react properly, he disappeared.

The toast.

The Singh parents (Brian's father did not look like Matthew except for the same blue eyes) both thanked the guests for joining in this celebration. The father acknowledged Faith's parents and her sisters. Then he turned it over to the best man.

Charity was beyond grateful she didn't recognize the man, but her sister, Hope was gazing at the tall, lanky man with clear adoration.

The best man gestured with his glass.

"To the perfect couple," he turned to address Brian and Faith. "I don't know what your other lives were like, but this surely must be your reward. You two were meant to be together."

Charity could barely watch as the man who so much resembled Matthew kissed her sister.

The best man raised his glass. "Here is to the Singh-Northquest union!"

Everyone lifted their glasses, Charity too.

The room erupted in more gaiety. The bridesmaids pulled the groomsmen to the floor to dance. Hope managed to cull the best man from the herd and pulled him into a sort of waltz.

Charity drifted to the edge of the tent. She was fine, just befuddled. It was too much all at once. But this was cheerful, not regimented. She took a deep breath. She'd figure it out. She had all the time in the world, did she not?

"'*No one puts Baby in the corner.*'" His breath was warm and raised the hair on the back of her neck.

"That sounds like a movie line."

"It is. I liked you better as a blonde. Didn't get the chance to tell you that."

She quickly looked around, the room swirled with color and movement. It hadn't changed. She was still here, in the right time or the correct time. *Oh hell.*

She still didn't turn around. He ran his hand down her arm and she knew she should pull away, but didn't. "'*The way I see it, if you're gonna build a time machine into a car, why not do it with some style?*'"

"How did you know?"

"I told you. I went back when I was eight, so I essentially grew up in the past."

She tried to pull away, but his grip was tighter than she thought. "But you can't go forward."

"You can't go forward; but you can go back," he purred. "Dance with me."

"You're the bad guy!" she protested under her breath, while following him to the dance floor. No one raised a single eyebrow at her dancing with a man not her immediate relative. She looked up into his eyes. They were just as dark and just as captivating as she remembered.

He wrapped his arm around her waist and pulled her to him. If he had indeed traveled here, he had not lost any appendages in the effort.

"Maybe I am bad. The Gods know my family is. But it turned out your Matthew was working just as hard for the Singh family as I was working for the Knights. Too bad those cheat codes were a non-starter, it was a pretty good idea."

"He used me."

"Girl from the future? Of course he did." Dranit whirled her around and then pulled her close again.

Betsy Nite, in the arms of a much cleaner and more reputable appearing Jacob danced past them. She glanced at Charity then stopped so suddenly she made her brother stumble.

"You're a Northquest?" Betsy started.

How could Betsy have recognized her? "Yes," Charity quickly acknowledged. "I'm Faith's sister. I'm so sorry I missed your lecture on time travel."

Dranit convulsively gripped Charity's hand.

"No one really believed my theory," Betsy admitted with a rueful smile. "Even with an advanced degree, it's hard to convince people to believe in the future."

"Tell me about it." Charity smiled at Betsy. "I'd love to have lunch with you sometime. Can I meet you on campus?"

Betsy looked surprised, but nodded. "I'll drop you a line."

Dranit moved them away. "Don't talk about it too much. No one will believe you."

"I don't even believe me. And do you want your money back?"

"No, keep it. I didn't know at the time what would happen. It could have been a useless notebook."

"Why did you return?"

"Find the girl, have the last dance?" He smiled down at her and she found herself responding.

"You must have surprised your mother."

"She said she always had an empty space in her heart, as if she had lost a child. So, when I showed up, she embraced me with no questions."

"Mothers seem to be pretty resilient that way." Charity thought about her mother ready to send her to the past, but holding back because of father and the rebellion...or Mirabella's mother, who sacrificed her daughter for the larger good. Yet that worked out. Mirabella said herself that she had a good life in the past. Not only that, she started a whole family dynasty.

"I'm actually somewhat of a heroic legend." Dranit spun her and pulled her back. "Turns out that all the useless artists in the family who were on call to hang out at the Duck and Screw were suddenly free. Made quite a difference."

"I don't even know if I changed things," she admitted, which was easier than confessing how wonderful Dranit's arms felt around her.

"You did." He stopped dancing. Their lips were an inch apart. The party raged around them, but she felt she was standing in a pool of silence.

"You changed me."

She opened her mouth, but no sound came out.

"I was ready to warn my grandfather about the tsunami, but I changed my mind."

"Why?"

"I'll make this easy, I say, 'I told you I would always come for you. Why didn't you wait for me?' Then you say, 'Well...you were dead—'"

"I thought you were," Charity interrupted him.

"'Death cannot stop true love. All it can do is delay it for a while.' You should see the film."

"When?"

"Whenever. We have all the time in the world."

About the Author:

Catharine Bramkamp is a writing coach and podcaster specializing in Newbie Writers. She is the author of hundreds of articles and a dozen books including *The Real Estate Diva* Mystery series, two essays in the *Chicken Soup for the Soul* anthologies, *Don't Write Like You Talk* and the poetry collection, *Ammonia Sunrise*. She holds two degrees in English, and is an adjunct university professor of English and writing.

She lives with her husband, Andrew Hutchins in Sonoma County and Nevada County, California.

www.YourBookStartsHere.com and www.NewbieWriters.com

Coming Soon:
Future Gold
(the sequel to *Future Girls* and Book 2 in the Future Girls Series)

The Morning Afterlife
by Sonnet O'Dell

eBook ISBN: 9781615725687
Print ISBN: 9781615725694

Young Adult, Paranormal
Long Story of 16,786 words

If remembering could bring about the end of everything, would you still try?

Karrin wakes up on the side of the road with selective memory loss; she knows her name and age but nothing more about herself. She walks the highway back to a town to find all but a few people have disappeared and that there are strange but beautiful beings hunting them down. It seems to her that some great apocalyptic event happened but she just doesn't remember it.

Karrin however is in more danger than she realizes as someone in her new group of friends is more deadly to her than those hunting them down. When she finds one of them, a young man roughly her own age named Gabe injured, she goes against all she's been told and helps him. Gabe in return wants to help her, help her to remember. Karrin's memories, however, could put her in even more danger and bring an end to everything she now holds dear.

Also from Eternal Press:

Weather
by Isobelle Winter

eBook ISBN: 9781615729456
Print ISBN: 9781615729463

Young Adult, Steampunk
Novel of 83,504 words

Loyalty will cost him everything he loves. Escape will cost him everything he is.

Julian Lambert has protected those with supernatural abilities from enslavement and death his entire life. But there is more to Julian than even he suspects, and when his own powers surface, he finds himself as much at risk as his charges. Now he's no more than a useful tool, with nowhere to hide from the hideous fate that awaits him. He's saved others, but can he save himself?

Visit Eternal Press online at:

Official Website:
http://www.eternalpress.biz

Blog:
http://www.eternalpress.biz/blog/

Reader Chat Group:
http://groups.yahoo.com/group/EternalPressReaders

Twitter:
http://twitter.com/EternalPress

Facebook:
http://www.facebook.com/profile.php?id=1364272754

Google +:
https://plus.google.com/u/0/115524941844122973800

Tumblr:
http://eternalpress-damnationbooks.tumblr.com

Pinterest:
http://www.pinterest.com/EPandDB

Instagram:
http://instagram.com/eternalpress_damnationbooks

Youtube:
http://www.youtube.com/channel/UC9mxZ4W-WaKHeML_
f9-9CpA

Good Reads:
http://www.goodreads.com/profile/EternalPress

Shelfari:
http://www.shelfari.com/eternalpress

Library Thing:
http://www.librarything.com/catalog/EternalPress

9 781629 291680